Luc and the

Lucy and the Big Bad Wolf

ANN JUNGMAN

Illustrated by Karin Littlewood

Young Lions

To Louis, loving friend and wise counsellor

First published in Great Britain 1986 by Dragon Books
Published in Young Lions 1988
Third impression June 1990

Young Lions is an imprint of
the Children's Division, part of
the Harper Collins Publishing Group,
8 Grafton Street, London W1X 3LA

Text copyright © Ann Jungman 1986
Illustrations copyright © Karin Littlewood 1986

Printed and bound in Great Britain by
William Collins Sons & Co. Ltd, Glasgow

2.15

One fine sunny morning Lucy Jones was walking through the woods singing happily to herself. She was wearing her new red anorak and carrying a bright red bag to match. As she walked along the familiar path, she stopped now and again to pick some wild flowers for her granny.

After a while, Lucy became aware that there was a constant rustling in the undergrowth alongside the path.

'Must be a rabbit or a squirrel,' she said to herself, and she stopped to pick some flowers.

'Wrong, wrong, wrong!' came a voice from the undergrowth. 'Not a rabbit or a squirrel, but a *wolf*!'

At that moment a large grey wolf leapt from behind a tree and blocked Lucy's way.

'Don't you recognize me, my dear?' asked the wolf.

'Can't say that I do,' said Lucy, putting the flowers in one hand and picking up her bag with the other.

'But you must, you must,' exclaimed the wolf.

'Well I don't,' Lucy replied, 'and that's that.'

The wolf ran along beside her. 'I'm your destiny,' he explained. 'Your fate. You're Red Riding Hood and I'm the wolf. Now do you see?'

'Not really,' said Lucy. 'You see I'm not Red Riding Hood. I'm Lucy Jones, wearing my red anorak.'

'Not Red Riding Hood?' said the wolf indignantly. 'Next you'll be telling me that you're not going to visit your granny.'

'No,' said Lucy, 'I *am* going to visit my granny.'

'That's more like it,' said the wolf, sounding encouraged. 'You're going to visit your granny and you're taking her a nice, juicy, delicious lunch in that bag, right?'

'Wrong!' said Lucy. 'I'm going to stay with my granny and grandad for six weeks because it's the summer holidays and I'm off school.'

'What's a grandad?' asked the wolf in a worried tone.

'A grandad,' replied Lucy, 'is a man who is married to a granny.'

'Oh,' said the wolf, looking confused. 'I never heard of a grandad before. Still, never mind. Let me see the lovely lunch you've got in your bag.'

'There's nothing in this bag but a few clothes,' Lucy told him.

'Now stop shilly-shallying, young lady,' cried the wolf. 'Accept your fate with dignity. Show me the old lady's lunch without more ado.'

'Oh alright,' sighed Lucy. 'I'll show you, but only because you're holding me up and I've got a bus to catch.'

She opened the bag and emptied the contents out on to the grass.

'A hairbrush, six pairs of knickers, some tee-shirts, a pair of jeans, a toothbrush, a dress and a book!' the wolf exclaimed in dismay. 'And where, I'd like to know, is your poor old granny's lunch, you cold and heartless girl?'

'My granny can get her own lunch,' replied Lucy, cramming her things back into the bag. 'Now go away, I've got a bus to catch.'

'I won't go away,' said the wolf as Lucy started walking again. 'What's the matter, don't you know the story? First I follow you to your granny's house. Then I

7

eat her up and then I eat you up as well, and the lovely lunch you're taking to the old lady. I'll eat you up in one gulp, little girl, just you wait and see.'

'Look,' said Lucy crossly. 'Be reasonable. You've made a mistake. I'm off to see my granny in London.'

'London?' repeated the wolf. 'What's London? Never heard of it.'

'London is a very big city. My granny lives there, and I'm going to catch a bus to the station and then take a train to London.'

'Bus?' said the wolf in a puzzled tone. 'Train? What do you mean? You're making all this up to confuse and bamboozle me, aren't you? Come on, Little Red Riding Hood, admit it. You're trying to escape your Fate. Come, my dear. Give in, accept the fact that you're going to be eaten by me and you'll feel easier about it. Stop all this nonsense about trains and London and buses. You're confusing me. The truth is that you're going to your granny's house in the woods and I shall follow you all the way there. I'm not stupid. You can't put me off the track that easily. I am your destiny and you are my dinner. You can't escape that. You won't shake me off. You just remember that wherever you go, I shall be a mere step behind.'

So the two of them walked on through the forest, the wolf running through the undergrowth and leaping out from time to time yelling, 'I haven't gone away! I'm still here! Wherever you go, there shall I also be,' and giving Lucy a wicked grin. Then he would lick his lips and disappear again.

Eventually Lucy came to the road. Cars were whizzing by in both directions. The wolf followed her on to the roadside.

'What are all those smelly, noisy things?' he asked.

8

'Cars,' replied Lucy.

'Whatever are they for?' asked the wolf in a disapproving tone.

'They take people around from place to place,' Lucy explained.

'Don't see why people can't walk like everyone else,' sniffed the wolf.

Lucy began walking along the road.

'Where are you going now?' said the wolf. 'You can't leave me alone with all these horrible things. I'm not used to them. I don't like them.'

'Well go back into the woods then,' said Lucy.

'And lose you?' exclaimed the wolf. 'No, my lovely, you won't escape me so easily. I told you, where you go, there shall I also be.'

'Well, I'm going to cross over the road on the overpass,' said Lucy. 'If you want to come too, that's your business.'

So Lucy walked up over the bridge and down the other side, and went and stood by the bus-stop to wait for her bus. And the wolf walked up over the bridge too, and stood next to her, looking suspiciously at the cars and lorries whizzing past.

'I don't like it here,' he moaned. 'Please take me back to the forest. You go to London on your own. I admit defeat. Please just take me home.'

'I can't do that,' said Lucy, 'or I'll miss my bus. Look, you go back on your own. Just go over the bridge and you'll be back in the forest.'

'Can't,' sniffed the wolf. 'I'm scared, scared of cars. Can't go back on my own.'

'Well, here's my bus,' said Lucy. 'If you can't go back, you'll just have to come to London with me.'

'Alright,' whispered the wolf, 'only don't leave me

alone with the cars, anything but that.'

So when the bus came Lucy got on, followed closely by the wolf.

'Dogs upstairs,' said the bus driver.

'I'm not a dog,' said the wolf indignantly.

'Did you say something, miss?' the driver asked Lucy.

'No,' said Lucy. 'Not a word. I'll take my dog upstairs.'

The wolf followed Lucy upstairs. 'What did he mean, calling me a dog?' he demanded.

'Look,' said Lucy, 'from now on everyone has to think you're a dog or you're in dead trouble. Now, you lie at my feet and no one will think you're a wolf.'

'I don't want to lie down on the floor, it's dirty,' complained the wolf.

'Be quiet,' hissed Lucy. 'From now on, never say a word except when we're alone. No one else must know you can talk.'

The wolf lay on the floor of the bus and groaned. 'What a life. I've got to pretend that I'm a dumb dog, and all I wanted to do was eat Red Riding Hood. What a turn of events. Oh well, fate and destiny play odd tricks.'

'Don't worry too much,' said Lucy comfortingly. 'It's only for six weeks. When I come back from Gran and Grandad's I'll bring you back to the forest.'

'Six weeks,' groaned the wolf. 'Six whole weeks. Forty-two whole days. In London with cars, and a granny I can't eat, and a Red Riding Hood who argues. What did I ever do to deserve it? I shall die.'

'Nonsense,' said Lucy. 'Now, not another word.'

Lucy and the wolf got off the bus outside the station.

The wolf looked round in confusion.

'There's nothing but houses and cars,' he complained. 'No trees, no grass, no animals. What kind of place is this?'

'This is a town,' explained Lucy.

'Is this London?' asked the wolf.

'No, silly,' said Lucy. 'This is a small town, London is a big city.'

'What's the difference?' asked the bewildered wolf.

'Cities are bigger,' explained Lucy.

'You mean, more houses, and more roads, and more cars?' demanded the wolf.

'That's right,' Lucy replied.

'I don't want to go to London,' wailed the wolf. 'I want to go back to my forest.'

'Well you can't,' said Lucy. 'You'll have to come to London with me – it won't be forever.'

'Cruel, unfeeling girl,' wept the wolf. 'First you pretend you're Red Riding Hood, and now you refuse to take me home. What did I do to deserve this?'

'I didn't ask you to follow me,' said Lucy. 'It's your own fault. You don't have to come with me if you don't want. I've got a train to catch. You can come with me or stay here, whichever you prefer.'

'Stay here?' exclaimed the wolf. 'On my own? Here, among all the cars and houses? No, don't even think of it. Promise you won't leave me here. I'll go anywhere, I'll do anything, only don't, don't, *don't* leave me here on my own.'

'Very well,' said Lucy. 'At least that's settled. You'll come on the train with me. But you'll have to pretend to be my dog. If anyone suspects that you're a wolf, we're in terrible trouble.'

'What kind of terrible trouble,' demanded the wolf.

'I don't even want to think about it,' replied Lucy. 'Now, when I say "heel boy" you're to cower at my feet. Do you understand?'

'I suppose so,' groaned the wolf. 'It's a good thing my old mother isn't here to see me. "Heel boy" indeed!'

'I'm just going to get a ticket,' said Lucy, and she walked over to the booking office in the station.

'Half return to London, please,' said Lucy nervously. The wolf opened his mouth to say something and Lucy snapped at him. 'Heel boy.'

The wolf crouched at Lucy's feet looking daggers at her.

'That your dog you're taking to London, miss?' asked the ticket clerk, leaning forward.

'That's right,' said Lucy. 'I'm taking him as a present for my granny. Come on, boy.'

So Lucy and the wolf walked on to the station platform.

'I'm hungry,' complained the wolf. 'If everything had gone to plan, I'd have eaten you and your granny and your granny's lunch by now.'

'Be quiet,' hissed Lucy. 'If anyone finds out you can talk we're in terrible trouble.'

'More trouble,' groaned the wolf, '*and* I'm hungry.'

A moment later a train rumbled into the station. The wolf began to quake.

'Whatever is it?' he whimpered.

'It's the train, of course,' said Lucy.

'I don't want to go on it!' cried the wolf. 'I didn't think trains were so big and noisy.'

'Don't be silly,' said Lucy as she climbed into a carriage.

Reluctantly the wolf climbed in after her. Lucy sat on a seat and the wolf sat opposite.

'You can't sit on that seat,' said Lucy.

'Fooey, who cares?' said the wolf, and he folded his legs and looked out of the window, singing to himself.

A moment later the door was flung open and in came the ticket collector. He looked at the wolf in amazement.

'You get off that seat, you great brute,' said the ticket collector.

'Shan't,' said the wolf defiantly.

'Did you say something, miss?' asked the ticket collector, scratching his head.

'Yes, I did,' said Lucy quickly. 'I said shan't, cos I don't think you should talk to my dog like that. Get down Rover, good dog, down.' Reluctantly the wolf got off the seat and lay at the floor at Lucy's feet.

'That's more like it,' said the ticket collector, 'but dogs aren't allowed in the carriages at all. That dog will have to go into the mail van.'

'Why?' asked Lucy. 'He's not doing any harm.'

'Not doing any harm? You call sitting on my seats not doing any harm? What *is* that thing anyway?'

'That,' said Lucy, 'is my dog Rover. Now stop being horrid to him, you're hurting his feelings.'

'Hurting his feelings? That ugly great brute! Don't talk so daft.'

'I'll bite your head off,' muttered the wolf.

'What did you say,' asked the ticket collector.

'Oh, I said we'd best be off,' said Lucy quickly.

'Yes you 'ad miss. All dogs in the mail van. So off you go and take that revolting dog away.'

Soon Lucy and the wolf were sitting on the cold, hard floor of the mail van surrounded by bikes and mail bags.

'I don't like roads and I don't like towns and I don't

like cars and I don't like buses and I certainly don't like trains, and most of all I don't like being called Rover,' complained the wolf.

'Sorry,' said Lucy apologetically. 'It's what the dog in my reading book is called, so it was the first name that flashed into my mind.'

'Well, it won't do,' said the wolf firmly. 'I'm a wolf, not a dog. I shall choose my own name.'

'Alright,' said Lucy. 'That's fair. Go on, choose one.'

'Can't think of any,' confessed the wolf. He thought for a minute and then he brightened up. 'I know, I'll call myself after this train.'

'Whatever do you mean?' asked Lucy.

14

The wolf groaned.

'You are stupid. Trains have names like "The Flying Scotsman" or "The Orient Express" or "Le train bleu" – fancy names like that. I know 'cos I read about it in a book.'

'Can you read as well as talk?' asked Lucy in amazement.

''Course I can,' said the wolf. 'Never mind that, what's this train called?'

'It's just the 2.15 to London,' said Lucy.

'That's alright,' said the wolf. 'Just call me 2.15 from now on. No more Rover.'

'2.15 isn't a name, it's a time,' Lucy protested.

'So what?' said the wolf. 'What's time to people is names to wolves. 2.15 may be nothing but a time to you, but to me it's a name. More than a name, it's *my* name and I'll thank you to remember that.'

'Alright,' agreed Lucy dubiously. But an hour later when they arrived in London, Lucy had got quite used to the idea.

2

Home

As the train rattle into London, 2.15 rested his nose on the window and looked out gloomily.

'Houses,' he complained, 'nothing but houses and streets and cars and shops and streets and houses. I don't think I'm going to like London.'

'Well, you'll just have to put up with it,' said Lucy. 'No one asked you to follow me out of the forest. The thing is, if you're going to live in the city and pass for a dog, you'll have to put a collar round your neck.'

'Collar?' snapped 2.15. 'What's a collar?'

'You have a collar round your neck and a lead is attached to the collar, and then I'll hold the end of the lead and you won't be able to run away.'

'But I don't want to run away,' explained 2.15. 'I don't like towns and cities and I don't want to be lost in one.'

'That's not the point,' replied Lucy. 'Dogs have to be on leads some of the time in London.'

'What are collars and leads made from?' asked 2.15.

'Leather,' said Lucy gloomily, 'and we haven't got any leather. String would do, but we haven't got any string either.'

'Yes we have,' said 2.15 helpfully. 'Look, there's string round all those sacks. Why can't we use that?'

'Because it's tying up the post bags,' said Lucy.

'Never mind,' said 2.15, and he took the string off the first sack. He stuck his head inside the sack.

'Hey, there's more string in here. Look, lots of

letters, all tied up with string,' and he began to pull all the strings off the packets of letters and throw the letters and postcards all over the railway carriage.

'Stop it, 2.15!' yelled Lucy. 'That's the post, the royal mail, you can't mess it all up like that.'

'But we need the string,' explained 2.15 as he started on the next sack and began to throw piles of letters over his shoulder. Some of them landed on Lucy like huge pieces of snow in a snow-storm. Within ten minutes the whole carriage was littered with letters, postcards and parcels, and an excited 2.15 handed Lucy 120 pieces of string.

'Is that enough to make me a collar and a lead?' he panted.

'Well, I certainly hope so,' said Lucy, looking with horror at the chaos around her. 'Now come here and let's see what we can do, cos we'll have to get off as quickly as possible when the train stops before anyone discovers this mess.'

As soon as the train stopped, Lucy and 2.15 hopped off the train. Just as they went through the ticket barrier Lucy heard a shout.

'Someone's been messing around with the post!'

Lucy and 2.15 heard the shout, but they went on walking as fast as they could.

'That's a very big dog you've got there,' said the ticket collector.

Lucy smiled sweetly. 'Yes, but he's harmless, wouldn't hurt a fly.'

'Just try me,' muttered 2.15 under his breath.

The ticket collector patted 2.15 on the head and they went into the station's entrance hall.

'You didn't have to say such horrible things,' snapped 2.15, glaring at Lucy.

17

'Like what?' she asked, surprised.

'Like about me being harmless and not hurting a fly and things – it's very upsetting for a wolf to be referred to like that.'

'Sorry,' said Lucy. 'But the main thing is that no one suspects you're a wolf. Now, let's sit down here and wait till my grandad comes to find us.'

'I don't want to sit down here,' moaned 2.15. 'It's all dirty. Look, cigarette ends, old bottles, cans, wrapping paper, bits of food, it's disgusting. . .'

'Now listen, 2.15,' said Lucy sternly to the wolf. 'You are not to say one word to my gran or grandad until we get back home. I'll have to be very careful and choose just the right moment to tell them that you're a wolf.'

'Not one word!' exclaimed 2.15 indignantly. 'That's not fair!'

'Don't be silly,' Lucy retorted. 'I've got to break it to them gently or they'll panic and call the police.'

'You mean I've just got to bark and lick their hands when they say "good dog" and all that nonsense?'

'That's right,' said Lucy.

'You mean I can't put your anorak on and say, "It's your grand-daughter Red Riding Hood, with your lunch"?'

'I wouldn't if I were you,' replied Lucy. 'My gran would thump you with her rolling pin if you tried that.'

'Then can I swing the door open and say, "Old lady, your last hour has come. Prepare to meet thy doom?"'

'I don't think you understand, 2.15,' said Lucy sternly. 'If you get found out we're both in big trouble, but particularly you – so you're to pretend you're a dumb dog until people get to know you and we can tell them the truth.'

'A dumb dog,' groaned 2.15. 'Is there no limit to the

humiliations I get heaped on my head?'

Lucy was just about to reply when she heard her grandfather's voice.

'Hello love,' he said, giving her a kiss. 'Glad I found you. I've been looking everywhere.'

'Hello, Grandad,' said Lucy. 'I had to travel in the mail van because of my dog.'

'Your dog?' exclaimed Grandad. 'What dog?'

'That dog,' said Lucy, pointing to 2.15.

Grandad looked at 2.15. 'What, that great lump?' he said with horror. 'What's your mum thinking of, Lucy? What are we supposed to do with a horrible great thing like that?'

'But Grandad, you've always liked dogs.'

'Not on the 17th floor of a tower block I don't, and anyway it's against the rules.'

'Oh please, Grandad,' pleaded Lucy. 'It's only for six weeks.'

'Only six weeks! Lucy, that miserable geezer next door, Pete Grubb, is just waiting for a chance to catch me out, and that 'ound of yours will give it to 'im. Still, come on, can't stand 'ere all day. Come on, we'll go 'ome and see what your gran thinks about it all.'

So Lucy, Grandad and 2.15 walked out of the station and took a bus to the High Road, and then they walked through the estate to Herbert Morrison Towers and took the lift to the 17th floor. Grandad unlocked the door and put Lucy's case in the small bedroom.

'There you are, love, in your old room, as usual.'

2.15 followed Lucy into the room and lay on the floor, his head on his paws.

'I don't like it here, Lucy,' he complained.

'What don't you like about it?' asked Lucy.

'Everything,' moaned 2.15. 'I don't like the dirty

19

floors of the buses, and I don't like the shops, and I don't like the lifts, and I don't like pavements, and I don't like cars, and most of all, I don't like people.'

'Well, you'll have to put up with it,' said Lucy. 'I can't take you home for six weeks and that's that.'

2.15 stood up and put his paws on the windowsill, and stared miserably out of the window. Grandad made some tea and Lucy went to sit with him. 2.15 lay at her feet looking more and more fed up.

'You'd better take that 'orrible 'ound for a walk around the park,' said Grandad. 'It's not fair to keep them all couped up. What does 'ee eat?'

'I don't know,' confessed Lucy.

'Well, what does your mum give 'im to eat?'

'Nothing,' replied Lucy honestly.

'Oh,' said Grandad. 'Feeds 'imself off rabbits, does 'ee?'

'I don't think so,' said Lucy.

'You don't know much about this dog,' complained Grandad. 'What's 'ee doing 'ere anyway?'

'I ask myself the same question, sir,' said 2.15.

''Ee spoke, Lucy! Did you 'ear that, 'ee spoke! Your bloomin' dog spoke!'

'Incorrect, sir,' replied 2.15. 'I am not a dog but a wolf.'

'A wolf?' shrieked Grandad. 'Get away with you, I never 'eard anything so daft in all my days.'

'If I can talk,' said 2.15, '(and can I talk!), then it's no dafter talking to a wolf than a dog.'

'Well, it's all very confusing,' complained Grandad.

'Confusing for you!' exclaimed 2.15. 'Then what about me? I live quietly in my forest in a story for centuries and then suddenly, in a flash, I'm on the 2.15 to London and real life. *Very* confusing, I can tell you.'

'What's 'ee on about, Lucy?' asked Grandad, bewildered.

'He's the wolf from Red Riding Hood, and he thought I was Red Riding Hood and he followed me because he thought I'd lead him to my granny's,' Lucy told her grandad.

'Oh,' said Grandad.

'Yes,' explained 2.15, 'she was wearing that red thing with a hood. . . .'

'My anorak,' Lucy supplied.

'Yes, that thing,' agreed 2.15. 'So naturally I thought she was Little Red Riding Hood and pursued her through the forest saying, "I am your destiny and you are my dinner." But instead of playing my game, she lured me on to a road and then I was lost. I had to come with her to London.'

'Look at the trouble you've landed us in, Lucy,' cried her grandfather. 'Why didn't you take the great brute back into the forest?'

'Cos if I had,' explained Lucy, 'I'd have missed the 2.15.'

'I wish you 'ad,' said Grandad gloomily. 'What your gran will 'ave to say about this when she gets in, I don't know.'

'Where is the old lady?' asked 2.15, cheering up, 'for she is my dinner even as I am her destiny.'

'Come off it,' groaned Grandad. 'Don't start talking posh in this house.'

'But I am a character out of a fairy story, you can't expect me to talk like everyone else.'

'It's bad enough you being 'ere without 'aving you talk all funny. And as for my wife, she's at work, and when she comes in I don't want you scaring 'er with all that nonsense about destiny and that.'

'I think you're being very unreasonable,' said 2.15. 'I've been waiting to meet this Granny for ages.'

Just then there was the sound of a key in the door.

'There she is now,' said Grandad. 'And you just mind your "p"s and "q"s or you're out.'

Lucy rushed to open the door and give her grandmother a big hug. Gran came in and put down her shopping.

'Hello love,' she said, beaming at Lucy. 'It's lovely to see you.'

'Good evening, ma'am,' said 2.15, bowing low. 'It's

an honour and a pleasure to make your acquaintance at last.'

'Oo'er,' said Gran. 'And who is this?'

'A wolf, ma'am, and your humble servant.'

Gran looked from 2.15 to Lucy and back again. 'Does he always talk like that?' she asked.

'I think so,' replied Lucy, 'but I don't know him very well yet.'

'Then what is he doing here?'

'I came looking for you,' said 2.15.

'For me? Whatever are you on about?'

'I am the wolf in Red Riding Hood. Your grand-daughter pretended she was Red Riding Hood and lured me out of my forest.'

'Oh,' said Gran, 'so I'm the old lady you gobble up, and then you dress up in my cap and shawl and specs.'

'Well,' said 2.15, 'I'm glad someone else knows the story.'

'Oh yes,' replied Gran. 'It was always my favourite story when I was little. But there are some problems. Even if I was prepared to let you eat me, which I'm not, I don't have glasses or a cap or a shawl.'

'I can see,' said 2.15 looking at Gran, who was really rather young as grannies go. 'It's very distressing to find a slim blonde with good legs, it spoils everything. I just don't know what to think.'

'Sorry about that,' said Gran. 'Would a nice cup of tea help?'

'It most certainly would,' said 2.15, brightening up at once. 'Thank you so much.'

'Don't you mind 'aving a wolf in your 'ome?' asked Grandad.

'Why should I mind?' asked Gran. 'He's got very nice manners and seems to like chatting.'

'I most certainly do,' said the wolf. 'It's been jolly lonely in my forest, particularly since the three bears left.'

'Well then,' said Gran, 'that's fine. I don't get many people to have a nice chat with these days. My children have moved away out of London, like Lucy's mum, and people don't talk to each other in these flats like they used to in the streets in the old days.'

'Quite,' agreed 2.15. 'Nothing is at all like it used to be.'

'I can tell you and I are going to get on a treat,' said

24

Gran. 'What would you like for your supper?'

'Anything ma'am, anything,' replied 2.15. 'I am not a fussy eater. Anything prepared by your own fair hands will be a joy and a delight to eat.'

Gran and Grandad and Lucy all looked at each other. 'This is going to be a holiday with a difference,' said Lucy. 'I can just tell that it is.'

3

A Dog's Life

The next day Gran went off to work and Lucy and Grandad were left to look after 2.15.

'What would you like to do today?' Grandad asked the wolf, and then added hastily, 'Within reason, of course.'

'Well,' said 2.15, 'since I'm in London, I would like to go to Westminster Abbey, the Tower of London, Madame Tussauds, Buckingham Palace and the Tate Gallery.'

'Come off it!' said Grandad.

'Typical,' complained 2.15. 'Typical. They ask you what you want and when you tell them, they say "no way". What a life!' and he lay down with his head on his paws.

'How do you know about all those places anyway?' asked Lucy curiously.

'I can read,' said 2.15. 'I may be a wolf but I'm not stupid.'

'No one said you were,' replied Lucy.

'Well, people assume these things,' said 2.15.

'Oh my gawd,' groaned Grandad. 'Not satisfied with bringing a wolf into my home, she has to find a wolf that can read.'

'I didn't know, Grandad, honest I didn't,' said Lucy.

'Where did you learn to read anyway?' Grandad demanded.

'Taught myself,' replied 2.15. 'I got very lonely in the forest when Red Riding Hood never came along so I took up reading. I used to sneak into the library in the forest and get books. They never understood how books kept disappearing and turning up again. I'm very well-read though, there are all sorts of things I know about.'

'Oh,' said Grandad, a bit bemused. 'Still, it doesn't help us very much. What are you going to do with yourself all day?'

'You don't have to bother much,' said the wolf. 'I see a road map of London up on your shelf – if I could borrow it, you would never see me. Piccadilly Circus, the Tower of London, the Planetarium, here I come.'

'Honestly 2.15,' complained Lucy, 'you don't seem to understand. You can't be seen reading in the street, you'd be arrested and put in the zoo. Outside this flat you have to appear to be a very ordinary dog.'

'I don't want to be a dog,' groaned 2.15. 'And I certainly don't want to be *ordinary*.'

'Don't you worry about that, mate,' Grandad reassured him. 'You're not ordinary, not in any way.'

'Thank you, sir,' replied the wolf.

At that moment, the front door bell rang.

'Into the kitchen, 2.15,' hissed Grandad. 'I expect that's nosey Pete Grubb from next door. 'Ee just loves to know what's goin'on, and if 'ee can get me into trouble, well, that would just tickle 'im pink.'

2.15 gave Grandad a long suffering look, but he went into the kitchen.

Grandad opened the door.

'Mornin', Pete.'

'Good morning, Bert.'

'Can I do anything for you, Pete?'

'Well, I got a bit worried about you because I keep hearing this strange voice coming from your place.'

'Well, what about it?' said Grandad. 'Me grand-
daughter, Lucy's come to stay. You know Lucy.'

''Course I know Lucy. Hello, Lucy.'

'Hello Mr Grubb.'

'But Bert,' continued Pete Grubb, 'it wasn't Lucy's
voice I heard. It was a different kind of voice, not at all
like Lucy. It was sort of posh and masculine.'

'Cor, you ain't 'arf nosey,' complained Grandad. 'Do
I have to tell you about everyone who comes to stay or
visit.'

''Course not, Bert,' said Pete Grubb, trying to peer
into the flat past Grandad's shoulder. 'I just wanted to

make sure you were alright. Still, you've got that big dog to look after you now, haven't you? I saw you bringing it in with you.'

'Oh, it's my dog,' Lucy piped up. 'You see, my mum's having a baby, so I brought the dog to stay with me here, because Mum's too tired to keep taking him for walks.'

'But it's against the rules to keep dogs in these flats,' declared Pete Grubb, pulling a small book from his pocket. 'Look, it's all down here in black and white, rule number 8d. "No tenants are to keep any pets other than goldfish and budgerigars." I'm telling on you, I'm going to the office right now to tell them you're in breach of the rules.'

'Oh please, Mr Grubb,' pleaded Lucy, 'don't get Grandad into trouble over 2.15. He only agreed to let 2.15 come and stay to help my poor mum.'

'2.15, 2.15? Whatever are you on about?'

'It's my dog's name. He was born at 2.15, so that's what we called him. I'll be taking him home as soon as the baby's born, and he's the nicest friendliest dog in the world. 2.15, 2.15, come here, good dog. Come and meet Mr Grubb.'

2.15 stuck his nose round the door and trotted out.

'Here dog,' commanded Lucy. 'Show Mr Grubb what a good dog you are. Shake a paw, go on, give Mr Grubb a paw.'

2.15 gave Lucy a pained glance, sighed, and gave Pete Grubb a paw.

'Ugly brute, isn't he?' said Pete Grubb. 'More like a wolf than a dog.'

'Like a wolf!' snapped Grandad. 'I can tell you've never seen a real wolf. Why, when I was in the army we went out on wolf patrols regular, and I can tell you that they looked nothing like this.'

'I did a project on wolves at school,' added Lucy, 'and they looked quite different. You can always tell a wolf, they have mangy tails and fluffy fur on their feet.'

2.15 glared at her and walked away.

'You'd almost think the brute could understand what you said,' Pete Grubb commented. 'Well, I'd best be off. Hope your dog licence is up to date, Lucy, and if that brute makes a noise at night or messes around my door, I'll be up to the council, quick as a whistle.'

'Don't you worry yourself, Pete,' said Grandad. 'You won't even know he's here,' and he shut the door in Pete Grubb's face.

'I do not like that person,' said 2.15 fiercely.

'Well, you're not on your own there, mate,' said Grandad.

'I suppose that if Pete Grubb is on our tail, Grandad, we ought to get 2.15 a dog licence,' Lucy suggested.

'I don't want a dog licence,' snapped 2.15.

'Well, that's too bad,' said Lucy firmly. 'You've got to have one. We'll go to the Post Office and get one, and then we'll buy a proper lead and collar and you'll be well set up.'

'You have the oddest ideas about what would make me happy,' said 2.15 as they went off to the Post Office to get the licence.

At the Post Office there was a long queue, and 2.15 began to get bored.

'Isn't there some way you can speed it up?' whispered 2.15.

Lucy knelt down as if to fondle him. 'Don't say another word,' she whispered angrily into his ear. 'People are getting suspicious.'

30

'Amazing, isn't it,' said the woman behind Lucy. 'At times you could swear they could talk.'

'Yes, I know,' agreed Lucy. 'It's almost as though he was trying to tell me that he was bored.'

'Next one please,' came a voice from behind the counter.

'I want a dog licence, please,' said Lucy politely.

'Looks more like a wolf than a dog,' said the counter assistant, leaning over to get a better look.

'He's a Great Alaskan Foxhound,' replied Lucy quickly. 'A sort of first cousin to the Huskies that pull sleighs.'

2.15 shot Lucy a furious glance as they left the Post Office and walked over to the park. When they got to the duck pond Lucy sat down and took off 2.15's lead. The wolf turned his back on Lucy and gazed hard at a tree in the distance.

'What's the matter with you, 2.15?' she asked, after checking that no one was within hearing distance. 2.15 just turned even further from her and stuck his nose in the air.

'Not talking,' he sniffed.

'Oh come on, 2.15. Why not?'

'You told the man in the Post Office that I was a Great Alaskan *Fox* Hound.'

'Well, I could hardly tell him you were a wolf, could I?'

'You didn't have to tell him I was a "fox" though. You could have said a Great Alaskan Wolf Hound or just a Great Alaskan Hound – I am very offended.'

'Sorry, 2.15,' said Lucy. 'No offence intended.'

'Well, offence has been taken.'

'Come on, 2.15,' said Lucy coaxingly, 'let's go for a walk.'

'Oh, alright,' said 2.15 grudgingly. So they walked along in silence until they came to a notice: '*All dogs must be on leads*.'

'I don't want to have a lead on,' sulked 2.15 as Lucy snapped the lead into place. They walked on a little further till they came to a lawn.

'Let's play ball,' suggested 2.15.

'We can't,' Lucy replied, pointing to a notice which read: '*No Dogs on the Grass*.'

'I can't believe it,' said 2.15 indignantly. 'Dogs aren't allowed to do *anything*!'

'I've still got some money,' said Lucy. 'Let's go and have something to eat.'

But when they got to the Park Café there was a big notice up saying: '*ALL DOGS TO BE LEFT OUTSIDE.*'

'It's too much,' complained 2.15. 'I've never been so insulted.'

'I'll get you whatever you want and we can eat it outside here, at the pretty tables with the umbrellas.'

'Can I sit on a chair?' asked the wolf.

'Of course not,' replied Lucy. 'Now, what would you like to eat?'

'I'll eat two jam doughnuts, a piece of strawberry cheesecake and a packet of Jaffacakes, please.'

'Is that really what you want?'

'Yes,' said 2.15, 'unless there's a notice up somewhere saying, "Dogs are not permitted to eat doughnuts, strawberry cheesecake or Jaffa cakes."'

'I don't think there's one of those.'

'You mean people let dogs eat what they like?'

'Yes,' said Lucy.

'What a relief,' sighed 2.15. 'Alright then, don't hang around. Off you go and get me my cakes.'

So Lucy and 2.15 tucked in.

'What's that you're eating?' asked 2.15.

'It's a hotdog,' said Lucy.

'I don't know how you can bring yourself to eat it,' said 2.15 indignantly. 'What did that poor dog do to deserve to get eaten? Walked on the grass, I expect.'

'Oh 2.15, a hotdog is just a name. A hotdog isn't made from dogs.'

'What is it made from then?' asked 2.15.

'I don't know,' confessed Lucy.

'In that case,' said 2.15, 'I think you should assume the worst.'

They finished their food and then began to walk home. They walked past the entrance to a tube station. 2.15 peered down.

'What's that?' he asked.

'It's the underground. You can get trains that go under the city.'

'I'm interested in trains since I'm named after one,' said 2.15. 'Could we go on one?'

'I don't want to,' announced Lucy.

'Why not?' demanded 2.15.

'I want to get home and watch the telly.'

'That box in the corner of the living-room which shows pictures?'

'That's right,' said Lucy.

'Well you can't,' said 2.15 firmly. 'You watch it far too much. Can't be good for you.'

'But 2.15, it's my favourite programme. And I'm tired.'

'Don't be silly,' said 2.15. 'Now come on.'

'Oh, alright,' said Lucy reluctantly and they ran down the stairs. 'Could I have a half return to Trafalgar Square,' she asked. 2.15 began to wander around and inspect the tube station.

'Is that your dog?' asked the ticket collector.

'Yes,' said Lucy.

'Well, you'll have to carry him on the escalator,' said the man. 'No dogs allowed on the escalator.'

'He's too big to carry,' Lucy protested.

'He can't go on the escalator, those are the rules.'

Lucy looked helplessly at 2.15, who suddenly pulled himself loose from her grasp and raced on to the escalator.

'I'll get him,' yelled Lucy to the ticket collector and she leapt on to the escalator after 2.15. He was waiting for her at the bottom.

'That was fun,' he said. 'I'd love to go up and down.'

'Come on, 2.15, let's get a train before the ticket collector comes after us.'

They waited on the platform for a few minutes. 2.15 looked at the advertisements. Suddenly he stopped. 'Just look at that,' he said. 'It's a disgrace.'

'Be quiet,' snapped Lucy. 'There are people on this platform.'

'Well look at it,' complained 2.15 in a whisper. Lucy looked at the offending advertisement. There was a picture of wolves lying at the feet of a beautiful woman in wonderful clothes and the writing said, 'Even wolves can't resist the scent of La Loup perfume.'

'That advertisement is an insult to wolves,' insisted 2.15.

'Never mind,' hissed Lucy. 'Come on, on to the train.' So they got on the train and 2.15 enjoyed the ride lying at Lucy's feet and watching everyone. When they got out at Trafalgar Square 2.15 admired Lord Nelson and then wanted to be taken into the National Gallery to look at the pictures, but they wouldn't let him in. 'No dogs allowed,' said the doorman. 2.15 was dispirited as they went down to the tube station to go home.

'Do you have a pen?' he enquired.

'Yes, why?' asked Lucy.

'Never mind,' said the wolf. 'Just give it to me or I'll start talking in a very loud voice.'

So Lucy gave it to him, and when they passed one of the advertisements showing wolves and no one was around, 2.15 wrote in large letters, 'This advertisement is an insult to wolves.'

When they got home, Gran and Grandad wanted to hear all about their adventures.

'It was awful,' declared 2.15. 'Couldn't go there, couldn't do this, couldn't do that. Honestly, it's a dog's life, that's all I can say.'

4

Grandad

Grandad and 2.15 sat together looking out of the window. All they could see was the other flats, a playground where the children were playing and the busy road with the traffic racing past.

'Not much of a life for you 'ere, is it, 2.15?' said Grandad.

'No,' agreed 2.15. 'Not compared with roaming free through the forest like I always have – though to be honest with you, it was a bit lonely.'

'Yeah, I can imagine,' said Grandad.

'Not much of a life for you either, is it?' said 2.15.

'No,' said Grandad sadly. 'Since I retired it's not been much fun. Gran goes out to work every day and there's not much for me to do. I look forward to Lucy's visits, but she goes off and plays with the other children or watches TV – I don't see much of her.'

'Where are your children?' asked 2.15.

'Oh, they've all left London – couldn't afford the house prices here. We go and see them and they come to us, but we don't see as much of them as we'd like.'

'When you come and visit Lucy's mum, you could come and visit me too and then I'd show you around.'

'That would be very nice,' said Grandad. 'Most civil of you, 2.15.'

'And maybe we could do some things here together till I go home.'

'Oh, I don't know about that,' replied Grandad doubtfully. 'It might be a bit risky. Still, let's think. We could go up to the allotment, you could run round up there.'

'What's an allotment?'

'It's a bit of land to grow vegetables and things on. You see, Gran and I used a 'ave a house with a garden and that, but then it got pulled down and we 'ad to move into the flats. I've never really got used to living up in the air like this, and I don't 'arf miss my garden. Anyway, I put my name down on the list for an allotment and got one by the railway.'

'You should live in the country,' 2.15 commented. 'In a little cottage with gables and a thatched roof like in the fairy stories, and you could grow things there.'

'Like in the fairy stories, you say,' said Grandad laughing. 'And I bet you'd like an old granny sitting in a rocking chair with little round glasses and a shawl.'

'Yes, that's it,' replied the wolf. 'Then at least we could get on with the story. As it is, I'm stuck at the bit where I say, "I am your destiny and you are my dinner".'

'I'd like the country,' said Grandad thoughtfully, 'but there's no chance of it. I'll end my days in this flat. Makes me sad, that.'

'I don't see why that should happen,' said 2.15. 'Lots of people move to the country. I roam about and have a look from time to time, and I can tell you that lots of folk have opened up tea shops and sell cakes and things, and they don't cook nearly as well as you. I think you should get a cottage in my forest and call it "The Red Riding Hood Restaurant and Tea Rooms" and sell cream teas and have a special wolf cabaret.'

'Nice idea,' agreed Grandad. 'Just a small matter of a shortfall of £20,000.'

'Leave it to me,' said 2.15.

'You worry me sometimes, 2.15,' said Grandad. 'You just don't seem to realize the danger you could be in. If the police get to hear about you, you've 'ad it, and old what's-'is-face next door is just dying to find out what's 'appening in this flat.'

'What's the matter with what's-his-face next door?' asked 2.15.

'I don't know,' said Grandad, 'I can't understand it myself. 'Is main pleasure in life seems to be gettin' other people into trouble. I call 'im Public Enemy Number One.'

'I think that makes him far too important,' said 2.15. 'I think we should call him Public Enemy Number Forty Nine, that puts him in his place. Now, let's go and see your allotment.'

Most days after that, if the weather was good, Grandad and 2.15 went off to the allotment and then stopped off at the pub on the way back. 2.15 liked the allotment and the pub because, as he put it, 'They had a good line on dogs. No "No dogs allowed" notices.'

2.15 was popular in the pub. People patted him on the head and gave him crisps. 2.15 liked crisps and he quickly learned that if he presented a paw and sat on his hind legs, or nuzzled people, he could get a lot of crisps.

'You really like those crisps, don't you, 2.15?' asked Grandad.

'Smashing,' agreed the wolf. 'I like scampi and onion best. I'm not so keen on the smoked bacon flavour or the plain ones but you can't be too fussy in my situation. You know, people are a push-over. It's so easy to get them to do what you want. All I have to do is present a paw and look daft, and Bob's your Uncle, I get a whole packet of crisps. There are times when I don't mind being a dog!'

At that moment they turned a corner and there was Pete Grubb.

'I thought I heard you talking to someone, Bert.'

'Only talkin' to the dog, Pete,' said Grandad hastily.

'But I heard someone answering you, going on about liking crisps.'

'You're hearin' things, Pete.'

'My hearing's perfect, Bert. You were talking to someone,' Pete Grubb insisted.

'Alright, Pete, I give in,' said Grandad. 'I'll tell you the truth. This dog is not a dog, this dog is a wolf and can talk because 'ee's not an ordinary wolf, 'ee's the wolf out of Red Ridin' Hood, see?'

'No need to turn nasty, Bert. No need to get sarcastic. I was only asking.'

'And I was only tellin', Pete.'

'Alright Bert, you win this round. But I'm telling you, I know there's something funny going on in your place, and I intend to get to the bottom of it if it's the last thing I do. You can't make a fool of me and get away with it,' and with that Pete stomped off.

'Well done,' said 2.15, chortling to himself. 'You told him the truth and he didn't believe a word of it, the silly man.'

'We'll 'ave to watch 'im, 2.15. 'Ee's bad news that one, a real misery and a kill joy.'

'Don't you worry,' said 2.15 cheerfully. 'He shall not outwit the wily wolf. Why did you tell the truth anyway?'

'I always *do* tell the truth,' explained Grandad. 'I've told a few woppers for you, but usually I'm dead straight.'

'What woppers?' asked 2.15.

'All about you bein' a dog and that.'

40

'Oh that,' said 2.15. 'Were you telling a wopper when you told old maggot-faced Grubb that you went out on wolf patrols?'

Grandad looked puzzled as he put the key in the door. 'Wolf patrols? What are you on about?'

'You told Grubb that you knew I couldn't be a wolf, that you'd know a wolf when you saw one because you had been on wolf patrols in the war.'

'Oh, did I?' said Grandad. 'The things I think of. No, I never even 'eard of a wolf patrol, I just knew it would flummox Grubb.'

'Were you really in the army?' asked the wolf.

'Not 'arf,' said Grandad proudly. 'Six years I were in it. I was seventeen when war broke out and I went overseas, Dunkirk, North Africa, Italy, D-Day landings, the lot. Trained as a commando, you see.'

2.15 was impressed. 'Gosh, that sounds exciting, tell me all about it.'

So 2.15 sat at Grandad's feet and heard all about Grandad's wartime memories. Then 2.15 insisted that Grandad pin up a map on the wall and 2.15 marked all the places Grandad had been to on it, complete with dates. Grandad was in the middle of relating one of his adventures when Gran came in.

'There I was in a dug-out with a few of me mates, while up above the enemy planes were bombing our positions. Then we saw tanks comin' towards us, and we thought we'd 'ad it, but me mate Shorty grabbed a grenade and quick as a flash. . . .'

'Oh Bert,' said Gran, 'not the war again. We've all heard it at least a hundred times.'

'Shush,' said 2.15 indignantly. 'I've not heard it before. I am totally intrigued and involved. I'd no idea Grandad was so brave and had such an interesting past.'

'Oh well, carry on then. Grandad's always dying to talk about it and we've all had it up to here, but if you want to hear all his old stories that's fine by me.'

'To me they're not old, ma'am, they're brand new and most diverting. Now please be silent.'

'Sorry I spoke,' said Gran, and she went off to wash her hair.

A little later Lucy came in from playing, and Grandad was relaying to 2.15 yet another of the dangerous scrapes he had been in.

'It was pitch dark, you couldn't see your hand in front of your face, when we heard the sound of gunfire. Boom, boom, boom, then it got closer. We tried not to breathe, then. . . .'

'Oh Grandad,' groaned Lucy. 'Not the same old stories *again*.'

'You go away,' snapped 2.15. 'I am finding Grandad's reminiscences very instructive and fascinating, and I am tired of constant interruptions.'

'Oh, sorry,' said Lucy, and she went back to watching television.

2.15 was so interested in Grandad's wartime tales that he got Grandad to go to the library and get him some books on the subject. 'I'd go myself,' he told Grandad, 'but there is a notice up outside the library saying "No dogs allowed".'

So Grandad got 2.15 lots of books and the wolf sat up late at night reading, and he always seemed to remember everything that he'd read. Each day Grandad staggered off to the library with piles of books to return and staggered back with another huge pile. On one of his trips Grandad bumped into Pete Grubb and all his books went flying. Pete helped Grandad pick them up.

'Never thought of you as a big reader, Bert.'

'Well, I'm doing some background readin' on the war 'cos the annual reunion of my commando group is goin' to be at my place this year.' said Grandad quickly.

'Oh, is that what it is,' said Pete Grubb. 'I thought maybe you'd got a mate indoors who likes reading.'

'No, it's just that me old army mates are comin' round, like I said.'

'Old army mates, eh? You must all be getting on a bit now, Bert.'

'Yeah, that's right, Pete. All either pensioners or comin' up to it, so we enjoy a get together, a few drinks, a few laughs, rememberin' the old times and fallen comrades. So if you get a bit more noise than usual,

Pete, it's just us old timers havin' a bit of fun.'

'O.K. Bert, just so long as I know. Careful with those books, now.'

When Grandad got in he put down the books and said to 2.15, 'We've done it now. Pete Grubb wanted to know why I'd got all these books out of the library and I told 'im it was on account of me havin' a reunion with all the other lads from the unit, 'ere in me own place. It was the first thing I could think of.'

'Well, I think that's a very good idea,' said 2.15 enthusiastically.

'I don't even know where 'arf of 'em are,' said a worried Grandad. 'You do get me into some situations, 2.15.'

'Not at all,' said 2.15. 'This is the perfect opportunity to phone up your ex-comrades-in-arms. All you have to do is say that you're in a very dangerous situation, that the enemy are closing in and sniping at you, and that you need their help. No questions, just to get over here at the appointed time.'

'Alright,' groaned Grandad. 'I just 'ope it's O.K. with Gran.'

'I'll make sure that it is,' said 2.15, jumping up and down with excitement. 'Go on, start phoning.'

So Grandad phoned around and managed to contact six members of his group, and they all agreed to come round the following Tuesday. Grandad refused to give anything away about the nature of his 'dangerous situation'.

'Just wait till they get 'ere,' he told 2.15 gloomily. 'When I tell them you're a wolf, they might go runnin' off to the police.'

'Surely they wouldn't tell on an old soldier?' asked 2.15.

'No, I don't think so,' said Grandad cheering up a bit. 'And it will be nice to see the lads again.'

So on Tuesday Grandad got in some crates of beer and lots of fish and chips, and Gran and Lucy arranged to go out and leave the flat free.

At 7 p.m. precisely the first of Grandad's friends arrived, leaning on a stick. Grandad sat him down and 2.15 bounded over to greet him.

'Nice dog you've got here, Bert,' he said, tickling 2.15 under the chin.

'How's the leg, Les?' asked Grandad.

'Bad, bad never really recovered from that bullet I picked up in Normandy. Haven't been able to work for years.'

'Sorry about that, Les,' said Grandad. 'Still, you get your pension alright?'

'It's a real problem,' said Les. 'I'm no good at paperwork, never was. Still, enough about me. What's this about a "dangerous situation"?'

'I'll tell you when all the others arrive,' said Grandad.

Soon six men had turned up and they were all delighted to see each other again. After a few beers they confronted Grandad. 'So tell us about the dangerous situation then, Bert.'

'Well,' said Grandad, looking uncomfortable, 'Well, it's a bit odd really, and I don't want any of you to think I've lost me marbles, but, well, the fact of the matter is that, eh, well. . . .'

At this point 2.15 jumped on to a chair.

'Gentlemen,' he said, 'the dangerous situation to

which our friend refers is none other than my humble self. Do not be alarmed that I have the power of speech. I am a wolf, but benign and well-inclined, and your excellent comrade here is under siege due to my continued presence under his roof.'

The ex-soldiers were pretty surprised at 2.15's speech, but once they understood what he was saying they decided on an answer to the problem. They began to hold a very large party with lots of noise to confuse Pete Grubb. They sang 'Lily Marlene' and 'We'll meet Again' at the tops of their voices, did a 'Knees up Mother Brown', and then told their wartime experiences as loudly as possible. 2.15 encouraged them, listening fascinated to all the memories and stories.

At ten o'clock Gran and Lucy came back and the party was in full swing. Gran said she'd met Pete Grubb and he'd commented on it.

'Good,' said 2.15. 'Now he'll stop being nosey about my books. '

'Do you really like reading all those books, 2.15?' asked Les with the bad leg.

'Gosh, yes,' said 2.15. 'You see, in the forest I didn't have access to a very varied library, so it's a real treat for me.'

'If you're so good at reading, are you any good at filling in forms?'

'Never tried,' replied the wolf, 'but I expect I would be. You come round here with your papers and I'll see what I can do. Two heads are better than one, or so they say.'

Then they sang 'Roll out the Barrel' and drank toasts to the unit and to Grandad and 2.15. Finally they went off home, after it was generally agreed that they should have got together years ago and they wouldn't wait until Pete Grubb needed to be routed before they met up again. They hurried off home leaving Grandad and 2.15 waving happily from the balcony.

5

The Wolf and Peter

Lucy went to the library each day for 2.15 to get him a supply of books and records.

'I do wish I could go myself,' moaned the wolf, 'You never get what I want.'

'Well, what do you want?' demanded Lucy.

'I don't know,' replied 2.15.

'Well then,' said Lucy 'how can I choose something you want if you don't *know* what you want?'

'Get me anything to do with wolves,' replied 2.15.

So Lucy came back with a book by Virginia Woolf, one by Tom Wolfe, a book about General Wolf and a record of 'Peter and the Wolf', telling the story in music and words of how Peter had outwitted the wicked wolf. 2.15 skimmed through the books that Lucy had brought and then informed her crossly that none of the people had anything to do with wolves, but had just borrowed the name. Then he settled down to listen to the record.

When it was over 2.15 said, 'Huh – I shall write my own version in which the wolf outwits Peter, and I shall call it "The Wolf and Peter".'

'Good,' said Lucy. 'I'd like to hear it.'

'Hear it?' said 2.15. 'With a bit of luck you'll both hear and see it.'

Later that day Les, Grandad's friend, came over to get 2.15 to fill in his form for his invalid pension. 2.15 got Les to listen to the story of 'Peter and the Wolf' and Les agreed that it was outrageous and very unfair to wolves. Then 2.15 studied the form, asked a few facts and then showed Les what answers to put in where.

Grandad was impressed. 'That's a very 'elpful talent you've got there, 2.15.' he said.

'Always pleased to help,' said the wolf. 'Anyone with a form problem should come to me.'

Soon word got round about 2.15's abilities with forms and people came knocking on the door asking for help and advice. 2.15 was delighted to oblige and swore everyone to secrecy about himself before he helped them. Within a week 2.15 had helped Gran and Grandad's son Fred with his VAT and the lady next door with her widow's pension, he helped one person with their tax return and another with a form for supplementary benefit, and he had assisted numerous others with car tax and insurance, driving licences, holiday booking

forms – in fact, the only form 2.15 did not fill in was a dog licence.

'You have to draw the line somewhere,' he announced.

A few days after 2.15's career as a filler-in-of-forms had begun, a strange young woman rang the doorbell. Grandad was by now quite used to a stream of strangers passing through his home and he chatted to her as he made her a cup of tea.

'My name's Liz Howes and I'm a social worker in this area. I've been hearing wonderful things about a form-filling-in genius who lives here.'

'Oh yeah,' said Grandad vaguely.

2.15 trotted over and sat by her feet, looking pleased with himself.

'Have I got it right?' she asked, a bit confused. 'This person does live with you?'

'Well, sort of,' said Grandad. 'It's a bit awkward to explain. You see, it's not a person really.'

2.15 nodded vigorously.

'Oh, is it you then?' Liz Howes asked Lucy.

'Oh no,' said Lucy, 'I'm useless at all that.'

'Then it's your grandmother?' asked Liz Howes.

'No,' yelled 2.15, leaping in the air. 'You've had all your guesses. It is me – I am the genius for whom you ask, ma'am.'

'My goodness,' said Liz Howes, and she put on her granny glasses. 'A talking dog.'

'Wrong, wrong, wrong!' shouted 2.15. 'Not a dog, a wolf.'

'Goodness, gracious me. But never mind,' she said, 'so long as you can fill in forms, I'm not bothered. I could do with some help in these flats.'

'You're telling me,' said 2.15. 'What a backlog I've

had to clear up. But Madam, to be of service to you would be more than an honour, it would be a pleasure.'

'Well, thank you,' said the social worker. 'You are being very obliging.'

'It's the glasses,' said 2.15. 'Your granny glasses. They remind me of the old lady I never got to meet.'

'Talking of old ladies,' said Liz Howes, 'I'm having great problems with Mrs Barton at number 118. She's hurt her leg and I can't get her a home help for at least a week. Could you help out there?'

'Madam,' said 2.15, 'your problems are over, and so are those of the old lady. Her wish shall be my command. I will look after her, and Lucy can do the shopping and all the things that might arouse suspicion were I to do them.'

'Wonderful,' said the social worker, and she went on her way feeling very happy.

So 2.15 started going to help Mrs Barton every day. He cleaned and cooked and tidied, and sat and talked with her for hours. Liz was delighted with her new assistant, and soon half the people in the flats were coming to see Gran and Grandad to ask for advice and help. Pete Grubb got angrier and angrier, for he simply could not work out what was happening next door and no one would tell him.

One morning 2.15 went off as usual to do his stint as a home help for Mrs Barton. He made her a cup of tea and they sat down and chatted together while they drank their tea. Mrs Barton told 2.15 that Liz Howes was going to be popping in that morning.

'Let's give her a surprise,' said 2.15. 'I'll dress up as you.'

'Why should you want to do a thing like that?' asked Mrs Barton in a puzzled tone. 'Oh, I see. You want to do it like in the story, like in Red Riding Hood.'

'Right,' said 2.15. 'I have been waiting for this moment for a very long time.'

'Well, come on then. Let's go and look in my wardrobe and find some clothes for you to wear.'

So 2.15 and Mrs Barton had a lot of fun finding some clothes. In the end, 2.15 put on a long evening dress that was forty years old, a hat Mrs Barton had worn to her daughter's wedding and carried an old handbag. Then 2.15 sat in Mrs Barton's chair by the fire. At about 11.00 the door bell rang.

'Who's there?' called 2.15.

'It's me, Liz Howes, the social worker,' came the reply.

'Just lift up the latch and come in, my dear,' called the wolf.

Liz Howes came in and saw 2.15 in his extraordinary attire. She laughed and said, '2.15, whatever are you doing in that weird gear?'

'You spoiled it,' said 2.15 angrily. 'You were supposed to say all that stuff about "What big eyes you have grandma", and while we're on the subject, lend me your glasses.'

'Well, alright,' said the social worker, digging in her bag. 'Here they are, but don't look through them. They're very strong and they might hurt your eyes. Sorry I didn't get the idea at first, 2.15. I'll go out and knock again, and then we can do it properly.'

So she went out and knocked again.

'Just lift the latch and come in, my dear,' said 2.15. Liz Howes came in.

'Oh grandmama, what big eyes you've got.'

'All the better for reading the small print on forms with, my dear,' said 2.15.

'Oh grandmama, what big hands you've got.'

'All the better for writing with, my dear,' said 2.15.

'Oh grandmama, what big teeth you've got.'

'All the better for eating scampi flavoured, cheese and onion flavoured, bacon flavoured, even no-flavoured crisps with,' said 2.15. 'Teeth come in useful for all of them.'

They all laughed.

'Oh dear,' said Mrs Barton. 'That wolf is a caution. I don't know when I last had such a good time, not since the Coronation.'

'Yes indeed,' agreed Liz Howes, helping 2.15 out of the clothes. 'I have found my work so much easier since 2.15 has been around. I don't know how you do it, 2.15, but you have solved so many problems.'

'Well, my dear,' replied 2.15 cheerfully, 'it just goes to prove the old saying, "Where's there's a wolf there's a way".'

2.15 became so well known in the block that soon he began to look after the children to give their mothers a few hours off. One evening five children were left at the flat.

'Off you go,' 2.15 said to the mums, 'off you go and have a bit of fun. I shall entertain the children while you are gone.'

'I don't think you should be left alone with five of them,' said one of the mums.

'Don't worry,' said Gran, 'I'll stay. I've got all the ironing to do.'

So 2.15 and the children played 'What's the time, Mr Wolf?' in the front room while Gran ironed in the kitchen. After a while Gran saw that they were having such a good time that they wouldn't notice if she was there or not. She asked 2.15 if she could go off and join the others in the pub.

'To be sure,' said 2.15. 'It is a pleasure and a delight to look after these children.'

So Gran went off and 2.15 ran a bath for the children. But while he was in the bathroom singing to the children, 'Who's afraid of the big bad wolf?' Lucy came home.

'2.15,' she whispered, 'Pete Grubb is out there and he asked who was looking after the children. He said he'd seen Gran and all the mums down at the pub. He says it's illegal to leave children alone and he's going to tell on us.'

'Oh dear,' groaned 2.15. 'Well, you go down to the

pub quickly and fetch your gran. Don't let old Grubb see you. I'll cause a diversion so he won't see you go in or out. You go out the back way and I'll make sure he's looking out the front all the time.

'Go and ring the bell next door,' 2.15 told one of the children, 'and then run away.'

So Maureen rang the bell and then quickly scampered back to the flat.

'Slam the door,' whispered 2.15. 'We want him to know it's us.'

Pete Grubb came out of his front door and, finding no one there, went back into his flat again.

2.15 said to another child, 'Your turn now, Doreen, we want to make sure he's in the front of the flats and not looking out the back. He mustn't see Gran coming back in. We can pretend she's been in the bath.'

So Doreen rang the bell and came back in quickly. They all giggled loudly.

'I'll get you lot,' shouted Pete Grubb from the hallway. 'I can hear you laughing in there. I'll get the law on you.'

When he slammed his door, 2.15 said, 'Your turn now, Sue.' So Sue went out and rang the bell and ran back in to the flat, and they all sniggered. Then there was a ring on the bell.

'Answer it, Hugh,' whispered 2.15.

So Hugh opened the door.

'Now you listen here,' said Pete Grubb. 'I've had enough of you lot, messing about ringing my bell all the time.'

'Only a bit of fun, Mr Maggot.'

'Grubb,' he shouted. 'The name's Grubb, and who's looking after you lot anyway?'

'Gran,' said Hugh.

'Well, where is she then?'

'In the bath,' said Hugh. 'She had a headache, she says a bath helps.'

'Well, when she chooses to get out of the bath, you tell her I want a word. And meanwhile I'll be watching the door to see if she comes back. It's my belief she's out and neglecting you kids.'

'*No,*' said Hugh. 'We're being *very* well looked after, thank you,' and he shut the door.

'Well done,' said 2.15. 'Any sign of Lucy and Gran yet?'

'They're coming,' said Doreen, who was keeping watch out of the back window.

'Right,' said 2.15. 'Your turn at the bell, Mike.'

'I'm scared,' said Mike. 'He's in such a rage.'

'Alright, I'll do it,' said 2.15. 'Tell Gran to go straight into the shower and then to answer the door with her hair wet.'

So 2.15 rang Pete Grubb's bell and scampered back in, quick as a flash. At that moment Gran came rushing in through the back door, completely out of breath. Maureen pushed her into the bathroom.

Pete Grubb began to bang on the door. 'Let me in, I'll sort you lot out, I'll get the law on you, I'll report that horrible dog, I'll get you thrown out of here, I'll. . . .'

Gran opened the door in her dressing gown. 'Whatever's the matter, Pete?' she said innocently. 'Whatever's got into you to make such a racket?'

'You were in the bath?'

'Well, where did you think I was with five children in the house.'

'Thought I saw you at the pub,' said a confused Pete. 'Sorry, must be seeing things.'

'Yes Pete, I think you must,' Gran said, and she shut the door. They all began to laugh.

'Thanks, 2.15,' said Gran. 'Well done.'

'Yes,' said Lucy affectionately. 'He saved the day.'

'Yes,' agreed 2.15. 'That was the story of "The Wolf and Peter", and I think the wolf came off best in that one.'

6
Superwolf

At breakfast one Monday morning Gran announced that she was on her holidays.

'Aren't you going away?' asked 2.15. 'I thought everyone went away for their holiday, and I think you need a rest.'

'Oh well, 2.15,' she said, 'I enjoy just having a bit more time here. I can go shopping and do some jobs in the house.'

'That is not a holiday,' said 2.15 firmly. 'You need to get away to the country or the sea and have a real break.'

'I'll take the odd day off to go and visit the children and that. One day we can go and visit my daughter Mandy in Harlow, and my son Sammy has got a caravan on Canvey Island – we could go there for the day.'

'Not the same as a real holiday,' insisted the wolf.

'Grandad doesn't like going away. He wants a cottage in the country or nothing.'

'I'll go away with you,' offered 2.15. 'We could go for walks and play in the sea.'

'Sounds smashing, 2.15,' said Gran wistfully. 'But I couldn't leave Grandad. We'll just have to hope that a miracle happens and we get our country cottage. Just a little place with a nice garden.'

'I'm working on it,' said 2.15. 'Just give me time.'

'What I'd really like to do this week,' said Gran, 'is go shopping. My niece Kathleen and my daughter Mandy are coming up to London, and if we could find someone to look after the children, we could have a nice day shopping.'

'You go ahead,' said 2.15. 'I'll look after the children. Lucy can help me.'

'There's a lot of them,' said Gran dubiously, 'and we don't want lots of trouble with Pete Grubb again.'

'He won't cause any trouble,' said 2.15. 'Not after he looked so silly the last time.'

'Well,' said Gran, 'I don't know how Darren, Karen, Sharon, Stacey and Wayne will feel about being left with someone they don't know very well.'

'Don't know very well?' said 2.15 indignantly. 'Does no one read to these children? A stranger indeed. If they know the story of Red Riding Hood, then they know me.'

'Yes, but even if they do,' argued Gran, 'they won't want to stay with you – they'd be scared of you.'

'Nonsense!' said 2.15. 'I didn't have any problems with the other children.'

'That's different. They knew about you before, being local, but Karen, Darren, Sharon, Stacey and Wayne have never heard about you.'

'I'll talk them round,' insisted 2.15. 'Just you wait and see.'

When Mandy and Kathleen arrived with the children there was no problem at all. Karen jumped up and down in front of 2.15 and said, 'Our Dad says you filled in his VAT form.'

'Yes,' agreed Wayne, 'and I was wondering if you could help me with my sums.'

'Are you the wolf who gets all the books out of the library,' Stacey wanted to know.

'Are you *really* the wolf out of Red Riding Hood?' demanded Sharon.

'My fame has spread far and wide,' said 2.15 beaming. 'Yes, indeed I am he; mathematician, gardener, intellectual, adviser to people and generally the most famous and helpful wolf in the world, and today you lucky children are to be looked after by me so that your mums can go shopping.'

'Hurray!' yelled the children.

'Told you,' said 2.15 to Gran. 'Alright, ladies, off you go and have a lovely day. Don't worry about us.'

So off went Gran and the mums, and 2.15 and the children stayed behind and had a lovely day together. After playing with them in the park and giving them their tea, 2.15 settled the children down in a small circle to listen to a story. He picked up a book.

'Alright, kids, this is your lucky day. Your Uncle 2.15 is going to read you a story.'

He glanced casually at the title of the book he had picked up. It was 'The Three Little Pigs'.

2.15 began to read the familiar story and the children joined in the chorus of 'I'll huff and I'll puff and I'll blow your house down.' When he finally finished the story 2.15 snapped the book shut.

'That,' he declared, 'that story was a load of old gubbins, and very unfair to wolves. I shall now tell you the true story of what really happened.

'Once upon a time there lived three fat, horrible, smelly pink pigs. They were so yukky and disgusting that you wouldn't have wanted to meet them, not even after they were turned into bacon. Well, one day these three revolting, utterly yukky little pigs were walking along the road when who should they be fortunate enough to meet but elegant and clever Mr Wolf.

' "Good morning, little pigs," said Mr Wolf, who had the most beautiful manners. "And where are you off to?"

61

THE THREE
LITTLE
PIGS

'"We're going to town to buy some materials to build ourselves a house," squeaked the three smelly, disgusting and thoroughly yukky pigs.

'Now the wolf knew very well that the three pigs were lazy and ignorant and stupid, as well as fat and disgusting and thoroughly yukky, and he knew that if *he* didn't show them how to build their house, they would waste all their money and effort. So Mr Wolf, despite the fact that he was very busy and on his way to a party, decided to show these three utterly revolting little pigs how to build a proper house.

'"What will you build your house of?" asked Mr Wolf.

'"Straw," piped up the first horrid little piggy-wig.

'"Alright," said the wolf (who as well as being elegant and polite and clever, was also a very good teacher and knew that the only way to learn was from your mistakes). "Alright, you go and buy some straw and build a house."

'So the first horrid little pig went and wasted some money on straw to build a house with. And who was it who sold that silly little pig the straw? Why, a man, of course. And did that man bother to tell the silly little pig that straw was no use to build a house with? No, he did not. Mr Wolf looked at the pile of straw.

'"Now you try and build the house," said Mr Wolf, knowing that the pig would have to learn from his experience. So he sat patiently while the first little pig built his big straw house.

'When it was finished, the silly little pink piggy looked pleased with himself.

'"Now go inside and see if it's strong enough," instructed the wolf. And the silly piggy obediently went inside.

'"Right," said Mr Wolf, "I'll huff and I'll puff and I'll blow your house down."

'And he huffed and ·he puffed and blew the house down. The pig stood in the middle and looked with amazement at the fallen straw, and he began to cry.

'"Don't you worry," said kind Mr Wolf, lending him a handkerchief. "It was all a learning experience."

'So the first little pig cheered up, and went off with the second little pig. They both went and bought some wood, and they built another house.

'"Will you huff and puff, please, Mr Wolf, and see if you can blow this one down," they called to Mr Wolf, who was going to be very late for his party. And kind Mr Wolf huffed and puffed as they had requested and, of course, down came their house. This time two little piggies were very upset.

'"Now, you just try and think what you can learn from this experience," said Mr Wolf.

'"I know," said the third little piggy. "Let's spend more money and build a brick house."

'"Now *that* is a good idea," said Mr Wolf. "I've got to hurry to get to my party. So here's some money towards the cost of the house, and on my way home I'll come this way, even though it's a long way round, and check that you've done everything right."

'So after having a wonderful time at the wolf party, Mr Wolf made a special detour to pass by the little pigs' house. It really looked like a proper house now.

'"Oh good," thought Mr Wolf. "Those three yukky and very silly pink pigs have got it right this time. I knew they would," and he knocked three times on the door. The three little pigs looked out of the window.

'"Hello Mr Wolf," they called. "Why don't you try to huff and puff and blow our house down."

'So poor, tired Mr Wolf stood in the road and called, "I'll huff and I'll puff and I'll *blow* your house down." And even though he had been dancing for hours, he huffed and puffed as hard as he could, but still the house stood.

'"You've done very well, little pigs," said Mr Wolf. "Now you'll be safe and sound."

'"But Mr Wolf," squeaked one of the little pigs, "there's a slate loose on the roof. What shall we do about it?"

'"Well, that's no problem," said Mr Wolf. "Just put this ladder against the side of the house, climb up and put the slate right."

'So each of the three little pigs tried to climb up the ladder, but they were all too pink and fat to get very far. So kind Mr Wolf nipped up the ladder and fixed the slate. But those horrid and stupid little piggy-wigs took the ladder away while he was up there, and Mr Wolf had no choice but to climb down the chimney to get down. While Mr Wolf was climbing down the chimney, the absolutely beastly little piggies even tried to light a fire, but they were too silly to manage it. So yet again Mr Wolf came to the rescue. He showed those three stupid little pigs how to light a fire, and then every day he came to fetch the pigs and take them for a run until they got thin and fit and could nip up the ladder as quick as one, two, three. And that, children, is the end of the true story of Mr Wolf and the Three Yukky Little Pigs.'

'I like the other version better,' grumbled Wayne.

'I liked 2.15's one better,' said Sharon and Karen. Darren and Stacey agreed.

"Course you do," said 2.15. 'It's much better *and* more accurate!'

Just after 2.15 had finished telling the children the true story of 'The Three Little Pigs', Gran came home and told him that the lady at number 107 was coming by to get him to fill in her Rent and Rate Rebate form. Then Grandad returned from the allotment and said he'd met a mate at the pub who was having a bit of bother with his street trader's licence and then Lucy arrived to say that she had been playing at her friend's and her friend's Mum wanted some advice about Child Benefit allowance.

'It's all go,' groaned 2.15. 'Alright, children, off you go with Lucy and watch television. I need the kitchen to myself.'

'You mean you don't mind me watching television?' asked Lucy in surprise. 'I thought you didn't approve?'

'In moderation, yes,' said the wolf. 'What I don't approve of is when you watch anything and everything, and don't ever think or read or talk to anyone. But as you have been out playing all day, you may now take the children and watch TV. Right,' said 2.15 to Gran, 'I'll just have a cup of tea and then I'll see the first problem.'

Grandad stuck his head out of the front door. 'There's going to be a lot tonight, 2.15. I can see three already.'

'Well, they'll have to wait outside the door in a queue. I'll get each one done as fast as I can.'

So a queue formed outside the door and 2.15 saw first one and then the next, like a doctor.

Pete Grubb stuck his head out of his front door. 'What's going on?' he demanded. 'What are you lot doing outside my front door?'

At that moment 2.15 stuck his head out and called, 'Next please.'

'It's that dog,' yelled Pete Grubb. 'He spoke! I don't believe it! I'll report the lot of you.'

'I think you're going a bit funny in the head, Pete,' said a woman. 'A talking dog, indeed.'

'You been drinking, Pete,' said another. 'You'd better go and lie down.'

'I heard that dog speak, he said "Next please". You must have heard him.'

'Rubbish,' said the woman. 'Bert came out and said "Next please", but not the dog. I'll take you round to the doctor's, Pete, as soon as I've had a word with Bert.'

'Come on, Pete,' said a man, 'I'll take you indoors

and you can lie down, and I'll get you a cup of tea. You're imagining things. I expect you've been working too hard lately.'

'I'm so confused,' moaned Pete Grubb. 'Ever since Lucy got that dog, life's been very odd,' and he allowed himself to be led back inside his flat.

7
A Wolf in Sheep's Clothing

'I am fed up,' announced 2.15. 'I am fed up at being with people all the time.'

'Well, who do you want to be with, then?' demanded Lucy.

'Wolves,' replied 2.15.

'There aren't any wolves in London,' retorted Lucy.

'Oh yes there are,' said 2.15. 'I know because I saw an advertisement.'

'An advertisement for what?' asked Lucy.

'Not telling,' said 2.15. 'I'll let you know when I get back,' and off he scampered.

'Where's 2.15?' asked Gran.

'He's gone to meet some wolves,' Lucy told her.

'But there aren't any wolves for him to meet,' said Gran. 'What can he mean?'

'Maybe he's gone to the zoo,' suggested Lucy.

'It's a long way,' said Gran thoughtfully. 'I don't think he'd go all that way on his own. Still, maybe we should take him to the zoo one day if he's missing his own kind.'

'Hmm,' agreed Lucy, 'but I don't think other wolves are like 2.15. They can't talk, and they haven't stepped out of fairy stories.'

'Well, the zoo is the best we can manage,' said Gran. 'I'll have a word with your Grandad and maybe we can get a party together and make a day of it. We could have a picnic, 2.15 would like that. We could take all the children 2.15 knows.'

'Sounds fun,' said Lucy.

'What sounds fun?' said 2.15 in a grumpy tone as he walked in the door with his tail drooping.

'I didn't see you come in,' said Lucy. 'You gave me a shock. I thought you were going to see some wolves.'

'So did I,' replied the wolf. 'But when I got there, there were just lots of nasty little boys tying knots.'

'Tying knots?' Gran repeated. 'Why, where have you been, 2.15?'

'I went to the Church hall up the road, St Peter's Church Hall. There was a notice outside which said, "A Meeting of the local Wolf Cubs". So I got all excited and went along, and what do I see but more people. It's too bad.'

'Oh, I see,' said Gran laughing. 'The Wolf Cubs. We thought you'd gone to the zoo.'

'It may come to that,' said 2.15.

'Don't look so miserable, 2.15,' said Lucy. 'That notice wasn't put up to confuse you. Wolf Cubs is a club for boys who aren't old enough to become Scouts yet.'

'I don't see why they have to be called *wolf* cubs,' complained 2.15.

'I don't know why either,' said Lucy, 'but I think it must be because wolves look after their children so well.'

'Jolly well do,' said 2.15, looking encouraged. 'And all the wolves in the pack help each other, it's not just every wolf for himself.'

'Then that would be why the Cubs are called Wolf Cubs,' agreed Lucy, 'because they do things together.'

'It's all well and good,' said 2.15, 'but it doesn't help me find the company of other wolves,' and, looking miserable, he began to flick through the paper. He browsed through the pages and then suddenly let out a

70

shout. 'Yippee!' shrieked 2.15 so loudly that Gran and Lucy nearly dropped their cups of tea.

'Now whatever is it?' asked Gran.

'I've solved my problem,' announced 2.15. 'It says here there's a Wolves Supporters Club, and there's a form here to join it.'

Gran laughed. 'Oh 2.15, that's got nothing to do with wolves. It's a football supporters club.'

'Then why is it called the Wolves Supporters Club?' moaned 2.15. 'It's most confusing.'

'They're the Wolverhampton Wanderers,' explained Gran. 'Wolverhampton is a town and the Wanderers are their football team, called Wolves for short.'

'Oh,' said 2.15 looking crestfallen, 'so the Supporters Club is all about people and not about wolves at all?'

'That's right,' said Gran. 'Never mind, 2.15, I'll cook whatever you'd like to eat tonight to cheer you up.'

'I'm not interested in food,' said 2.15. 'I appreciate the thought, but I'm not hungry, just lonely.'

'Gran thought we could all go to the zoo one day,' said Lucy, trying to cheer the wolf up. 'There's lots of wolves there.'

'I know,' said 2.15. 'I read about zoos in a book. They lock animals up in cages so that people can look at them.' He shuddered. 'I'd hate to be in a zoo.'

'Don't worry about that,' said Gran. 'If you're careful, you never will be.'

'Provided Public Enemy Number Forty Nine doesn't rumble me, I don't suppose I will,' agreed 2:15. 'If we go to the zoo, I can talk wolf talk to the wolves there, can't I?'

'You certainly can,' agreed Lucy. 'And as soon as Grandad comes in, we'll arrange a whole day at the zoo.'

So 2.15 felt better and asked for a prawn cocktail, to be followed by steak, jacket potatoes and salad, and a peach melba for his supper.

'We'll have a feast,' he told Gran. 'A feast to celebrate our decision to go to the zoo.'

As they finished their meal, 2.15 proposed a toast. 'To Gran, Grandad, The Wolves Supporters Club, Wolf Cubs and wolves everywhere.' They clinked their glasses and drank the wine.

From that day on 2.15 became a dedicated Wolves Supporter and read the sports pages every day to see what his team was up to. He watched every sports programme to see if he could pick up any news of the Wolves. One day he was nearly beside himself because Wolves were coming to play a match with the local team.

'Well, what of it?' asked Grandad when 2.15 told him the news.

'They'll be playing only a few stops away on the tube – we can go and see Wolves play and I can wear my supporter's scarf.'

'What are you on about, 2.15? Honestly, you do get the daftest ideas. No dogs are allowed inside the football stadium.'

'I know,' said 2.15, 'but I could borrow some of your clothes and pretend to be a person. I'm taller than you if I stand up.'

'Come off it,' said Grandad firmly. 'There is no way, absolutely no way I will go to a football match with you togged up in my clothes – so you just forget it, 2.15. Alright?'

'Not alright,' grumbled the wolf. 'I don't ask for much, just to be taken to a football match occasionally. Still, don't mind me, I'll just fill in forms and look after the children, and help everyone and never have any fun. But I'll be alright, don't you worry about me. If my request is unreasonable, so be it. I had some illusions that you were my friend but that seems to have been a mistake. Still, I put it down to my lack of experience of the world. A few more weeks of contact with people and I'll learn what to expect. I'll know that people won't help out a lonely wolf even though he doesn't ask for much and. . .'

'Oh 2.15, come off it,' said Grandad, covering his ears. 'How long are you goin' to go moanin' and complainin' and bein' sorry for yourself?'

"Till you agree to take me to the football match,' replied the wolf.

'Oh alright,' said Grandad. "Ave it your own way, but on your 'ead be it. If you end up in the zoo, don't go blamin' me.'

'Never, dear sir, never,' said 2.15, beaming with delight at the thought of seeing his team in action.

So on Saturday, Grandad and 2.15 set off for the football match. 2.15 was dressed in a pair of Grandad's trousers, a polo necked sweater and a huge sheepskin jacket, with a cloth cap and gloves and boots and a Wolves supporter's scarf covering his face.

'I'm a wolf in sheep's clothing,' he told Gran proudly.

'I think you're crazy, 2.15,' said Gran. 'You're taking such a risk.'

'Nonsense, ma'am, no risk. I shall just use my charm and intelligence to talk my way out of trouble, and if that fails I can always run for it.'

Grandad and 2.15 found their way to their seats just before the game began. The match was very exciting and no one took any notice of 2.15. When the game was over, 2.15 said to Grandad, 'There, I told you there was

no reason to worry so much. Your anxieties, your fears for the well-being of my person. . . .'

'I wouldn't be too sure of about that,' groaned Grandad. 'Look who's coming towards us.'

2.15 looked up to see Pete Grubb pushing his way through the crowd towards them.

'Don't you worry about a thing,' said 2.15 to Grandad. 'Leave it all to me. I'll deal with this entirely alone and unaided.'

'Hello, Bert,' said Pete Grubb, looking hard and suspiciously at 2.15. 'I didn't know you were a football fan.'

'There's a lot of things you don't know about me,' said Grandad.

'So I'm beginning to think,' said Pete Grubb. 'Who's your friend?'

'Wolf,' said 2.15. 'Myron J. Wolf, Junior, of New York City in the good old U S of A. I'm mighty pleased to meet you, sir.'

'Yes, er, Myron,' said Grandad, who was more than a bit surprised. 'This is my neighbour, Pete Grubb.'

2.15 took Pete Grubb's hand and shook it energetically.

'Pete Grubb, well really, what extraordinary names you English do have. But I sure am mighty pleased to meet you, Mr Maggot.'

'Grubb,' snapped Pete Grubb.

'I am so sorry,' said 2.15. 'I do have the most terrible memory for names, and also I have toothache, hence the scarf covering my face.'

'Oh, is that what it's for?' said Pete Grubb.

'Oh yes indeedee,' insisted 2.15. 'Would you like me to show you the offending tooth?'

Pete Grubb stepped back in horror, 'Oh no, Mr Wolf, don't bother. I'll be off then. See you, Bert.'

'Right, see yer, Pete,' said Grandad looking relieved.

'Mr Insect, it has been a pleasure meeting you, and I want to tell you that I think your English policemen are wonderful, and I just *love* your funny old football matches, and if you're ever in the good old U S of A, don't hesitate to look me up. Just a moment and I'll find you my card. Hang on, I must have one somewhere with my address on. . . .'

'Very kind I'm sure, Mr Wolf,' said Pete Grubb, 'but not to worry, I must be off,' and he disappeared into the crowd.

'Told you I could handle it,' said 2.15.

'You did that alright,' chuckled Grandad. 'Well done, Myron J. Wolf Junior.'

'Come on,' said 2.15, 'let's go home and tell Gran and

Lucy and give them a laugh.'

So Grandad and 2.15 hurried home and were in the middle of telling Gran and Lucy when there was a loud knock at the door.

'Quick,' Grandad hissed at 2.15. 'Get those clothes off. . . Coming!' he yelled at the door.

2.15 ran into the bedroom and quickly took the clothes off, hanging the jacket up and putting the shoes tidily under the bed, and folding the socks and gloves and popping them in the drawer. Grandad opened the front door and there stood two policemen.

'Excuse me, sir,' said one. 'Sorry to bother you, but we are looking for an escaped criminal and we have received information that he may be staying here.'

'Staying here?' said Grandad in amazement.

'Well, yes sir. We received information that a strange man is staying in your flat. A neighbour has been hearing a strange male voice here for some days now. Our information says that this man never goes out and that you deny he's here.'

'No one here, officer. Just myself, me wife and me grand-daughter, Lucy and 'er dog.'

2.15 bounded out of the bedroom and licked the policeman's hand. The policeman patted him on the head.

'That's a very nice dog you've got there,' said the policeman.

'Yeah,' agreed Grandad. 'He'd keep any villain away. Still, officer, if you want to search my flat, go ahead. I've got nothing to hide.'

'If you don't mind, sir, just another few questions. Our informant also said that you were seen at a football match this afternoon with a very strange American called, er, Myron J. Wolf, and that this Mr Wolf was acting very strangely. Do you know where Mr Wolf is

76

now, sir?'

2.15 sat at Grandad's feet and buried his head in his paws, trying not to laugh.

'Oh, I expect he's somewhere around,' said Grandad vaguely. 'You're never quite sure about Myron from one minute to the next.'

'Would you like a cup of tea?' asked Gran.

'Yes please,' said the policemen, and after they had drunk their tea and 2.15 had persuaded them to give him all their biscuits, they apologized to Grandad for bothering him and left.

'That Pete Grubb,' said Grandad, ''ee'll stop at nothing.'

'Tonight,' said 2.15, 'I shall sing in the bath and that will really confuse old maggot, who probably got told off by the police for wasting their time. He'll be kept up all night wondering what's going on, and there's not a thing he can do.'

8
3.45

After his trip to the football match, 2.15 began to want to go out more and more.

"Ee's going to get caught if 'ee carries on like this,' said Grandad. 'I wish 'ee'd calm down and stay indoors.'

But 2.15 would have none of it, and on Sunday afternoon he announced that there was a fair on Hampstead Heath and that he was going to take Lucy.

'I don't want to go to the fair,' complained Lucy. 'All those things going round and round, they make me sick. And there's a good film I want to watch on the telly.'

'None of that, dear child,' said 2.15 severely. 'None of that. Come on now, put on your anorak and off we go. Come on or I'll go on my own.'

'You'd better go with 'im, Lucy,' said her grandfather. 'It's not safe for 'im to go on 'is own.'

'Oh alright,' groaned Lucy, 'but you'd better behave, 2.15, or I'll be very cross.'

'My dear girl,' said 2.15, 'what a statement. When have I not behaved?'

So off they went with £10 to pay for their tube tickets and for the fair itself. As soon as they arrived 2.15 caught sight of the Big Dipper.

'Let's go on that,' he said excitedly.

'Oh no,' groaned Lucy. 'It makes me sick.'

'Come on,' said 2.15. 'You won't be sick. It's all in your head.'

So Lucy paid and they got on.

'Hey!' yelled the man in charge just as the Big Dipper began to move off. 'No dogs allowed!'

2.15 merely waved and away they went. 2.15's whoops of delight were drowned by the shrieks and cries of other people on the Big Dipper.

When the ride was over and they were getting off, the man shouted at Lucy, 'And don't you ever bring that horrible big dog on here again!'

'That was good,' said 2.15 to Lucy, 'I enjoyed that.'

'I didn't like getting shouted at,' complained Lucy.

'I'll make it up to you,' promised the wolf. 'Come on, let's go on that,' and he pointed at the Big Wheel. So reluctantly Lucy paid, and 2.15 leaped in next to her just at the ride started.

'No animals allowed!' shouted the Big Wheel operator as they disappeared from view. When the machine stopped, they jumped out and ran quickly out of sight. They stopped when they came to the bumper cars.

'Those look fun,' said 2.15, who was having a wonderful time and getting very excited. 'This has got filling in forms beaten every time.'

So Lucy bought a ticket and 2.15 got in next to her. Lucy drove around rather timidly, trying not to get bumped into.

'That's not the way to do it,' said the wolf, and he grabbed the steering wheel and drove as hard as he could into as many people as he could, whooping and shouting as he did so. 2.15 thought it was great.

'Let's have another go,' he shouted. But the man who ran the bumper cars was jumping from car to car. He grabbed hold of Lucy.

'Alright you, 'op it, and don't bring that loony dog of yours on my cars again. You must be barmy, bringing a dog to a fair.'

'Not to worry,' said 2.15 cheerfully as they walked away.

'Well, I'm fed up of being shouted at because of you,' retorted Lucy.

'Tell you what,' said 2.15. 'Let's get some candy floss and then have a go on the swings and tombola, and then we can go home.'

'Promise we can go after that,' said Lucy firmly.

'Promise,' said 2.15. 'Wolf's honour.'

So they ate some candy floss and then went on the swings. 2.15 won some goldfish in the tombola.

'Time to go now,' said Lucy.

'But I'm having such a good time,' said the wolf wistfully. 'For years I've watched when the fair came to the forest, and now I've been able to join in.'

'You promised, 2.15,' said Lucy angrily, 'And anyway, I haven't got any money left, just enough for the fare home on the bus.'

'I suppose I'll have to come,' moaned 2.15, 'but I'm so hungry. Can I have some packets of crisps.'

'No, 2.15,' Lucy explained. 'Look, just enough money for the fare home.'

'Hmm,' said the wolf, and as they passed a stall he grabbed two packets of crisps and gobbled them down. The woman running the stall dashed out and grabbed Lucy.

'You should keep that dog of yours on a lead, he nicked two packets of crisps. Now you just hand over the money.'

So Lucy gave the woman all her fare money. 'That was a rotten thing to do, 2.15,' complained Lucy, nearly in tears. 'Now how are we going to get home?'

'Well, we could walk,' suggested 2.15.

'It's too far,' replied Lucy, 'and I don't know the way.'

'It's all my fault,' said 2.15. 'But let's not panic. Let's try and think of a way out of the problem. I know, I will be a performing dog. You tell me to do things and I'll do them, then we'll collect some money in a hat.'

'I haven't got a hat,' protested Lucy.

'There's a paper one on the ground over there,' said 2.15. 'Someone dropped it. I'll go and get it.'

When 2.15 came back with the hat, they went to a tea place and began the show.

'Stand on a chair and say in a loud voice, "This is the

Lucy Jones and Her Amazing Performing Dog Show".'

'I can't,' whispered Lucy, 'I feel too embarrassed.'

'Alright,' said 2.15 cheerfully. 'Let's start walking home.'

So Lucy reluctantly got on the chair and made the announcement and asked people to give 2.15 instructions. One woman told him to pick up her gloves and he did, then a man told him to go and lick the waitress's foot and he did, and then another told 2.15 to put a menu in a basket which he did. After half an hour of obeying instructions for the appreciative crowd, Lucy gave 2.15 the hat and told him to collect the money. So 2.15 trotted round with the hat in his mouth and they got a lot of money.

'Enough for the bus fare home *and* some crisps,' whispered 2.15.

At that moment Lucy caught sight of Pete Grubb pushing his way through the crowd.

'Heel dog,' she snapped at 2.15 who was still collecting money. 2.15 sat down and Lucy put his lead on.

'Oh, hello Mr Grubb,' she said in a surprised voice as he approached. 'We don't seem to be able to get away from you anywhere.'

'So it would seem,' said Pete Grubb. 'Got a Street Performer's Permit have you, for your little show with your dog?'

'I didn't know you needed one,' said Lucy.

'Oh yes,' said Pete Grubb smiling broadly. 'I shall have to tell the law that you've been performing without the necessary authorisation if I see you and that hound at it again,' and off he went.

'What a spoil sport,' groaned 2.15. 'I wonder why he's like that?'

'Well, never mind about him,' said Lucy. 'I'm

exhausted and I want to go home.'

On the way home, 2.15 commented to Lucy, 'We could make lots of money, you know. Whenever we need money we'll just give a little show. People think dogs are stupid, and they can't believe that I understand what they say.'

'Well, I don't know about it, 2.15,' said Lucy doubtfully. 'Now that we've got Pete Grubb on our backs again, maybe we'd better not.'

'My dear girl,' said 2.15, 'my very dear girl, you worry too much.'

After his trip to the fair, 2.15 got even more keen on going out and increasingly confident about taking trips and travelling around. 'All I do is jump on a bus after someone and go upstairs,' he explained to Gran. 'No one ever asks who I'm with, and I just get off when I get to my destination. And if the tube seems to be more convenient, I just run down the escalators and let them think I'm a stray. I can go anywhere I like, the Tower of London, Buckingham Palace, Westminster Abbey, anywhere.'

Gran and Grandad were worried.

'2.15 is getting too big for his boots,' said Gran. 'He's not being at all careful. If he goes on like this he'll get caught.'

'I know, love,' agreed Grandad. 'Maybe it's time 'ee thought of goin' 'ome.'

'I will miss him though,' said Gran.

'Me too,' said Grandad sadly. 'But it's for 'is own good.'

'Yes,' agreed Gran, wiping away a tear. 'But there'll be no one to have a natter and a laugh with, no one to baby sit and fill in all those forms. Still, he can't stay for ever so it might as well be now.'

'We'd better talk to 'im, I suppose,' said Grandad.

'Explain to 'im that it's for 'is own good. 'Ee's a reasonable chap, I mean, wolf.'

'Yes,' said Gran. 'That would be the way to do it, and then we'll arrange for someone to drive him back to his home. He's much safer in his own forest.'

When 2.15 came back from his day of sight-seeing he was tired but happy, and he told Gran all about his trip up the Thames.

'I just got on a boat at Tower Pier and wandered about. No one asked who I belonged to. Jolly interesting, the history of the Thames. When we got to Hampton Court I got off and looked around, interesting maze and kitchens there, and the architecture was beautiful. I wished I could have asked the guide some questions. So I went around a few times and then hopped on a bus, and then changed on to a tube and here I am, no trouble and it didn't cost me a penny.'

'Well, 2.15,' said Grandad, 'Gran and me 'ave been talkin' and we think it, er, well, you know, it might be like, a bit, sort of – well, we think that you might get into a lot of trouble if you stay in London. We worry about you wanderin' around the way you do, and there's Pete Grubb next door just waitin' to get you – we think it's time you went 'ome to your forest.'

'Not yet!' said 2.15 indignantly. 'Just when I've begun to find my way around and have a good time.'

'We'll be sorry to see you go,' said Gran. 'Honest 2.15, it's lovely having you around, but when you go off like this I do worry.'

'What about?' demanded 2.15.

'You ending up in the zoo, of course,' replied Grandad.

'And talking of the zoo,' said the wolf, 'when are you going to take me there for my picnic?'

'What picnic?' said Grandad.

'The one at the zoo that you promised me,' explained 2.15 patiently. 'To meet some of my own kind.'

'Oh yes,' said Gran. 'You remember, love, when 2.15 was looking for some wolves to be friendly with.'

'Oh yeah,' said Grandad. 'That's right, we did promise. Alright then, we'll go on Friday, with Lucy and some of the kids from the flats. It can be your treat, 2.15, before you go back to the forest.'

So on Friday they all set off with a big picnic hamper. They went on the bus and then they walked through Regent's Park. Gran went and bought the tickets, but she was told that 2.15 could not get in as no dogs were allowed.

'Alright, you take the children in, love,' said Grandad. 'I'll take poor old 2.15 for a walk round and we'll meet you back here for the picnic at 4 o'clock.'

So off they went, leaving Grandad to cope with a very disgruntled 2.15.

'It's typical,' he complained bitterly to Grandad, 'It's typical of people to lock all those poor animals up in cages, and then not allow other animals in to see them.'

'Never mind, old chap,' said Grandad. 'You and me'll take a walk instead, and I'll get you an ice cream and some crisps.'

So they set off round the park. Suddenly 2.15 stopped and pricked up his ears, then he threw back his head and let out a wolf's howl. Grandad was appalled.

'Shut up, 2.15,' he said sharply. 'People are looking.'

'Blow people,' said 2.15 and went on howling.

In the distance came an answering call.

'It's another wolf,' said Grandad. 'That's right, I remember now, the wolves are on the outside of the zoo, next to the park.'

2.15 took off and Grandad followed as fast as he

86

could. When Grandad got to the wolf section, there was 2.15 jumping up and down and making noises, while another wolf stood inside the railings of the zoo howling back. Grandad ran up to 2.15 and grabbed the wolf by the collar.

'Whatever are you doin', 2.15?' he asked breathlessly.

'What's the time?' asked 2.15 dreamily.

'3.45,' said Grandad in a surprised tone. 'What's that got to do with anything?'

'Then that's her name,' announced 2.15. 'I shall call her 3.45 after the moment when our eyes met, and our promise of true love was sealed forever.'

'Whatever are you on about?' asked Grandad.

'That,' said 2.15, pointing to the wolf inside the enclosure, 'is 3.45. She and I are in love, and we're going to get married and live happily ever after.'

'But 2.15, she's in the zoo and you're out here.'

'I know,' said 2.15, 'but I've got a little plan.' And he blew a kiss to the wolf in the cage. 'Farewell, dear heart. Parting is such sweet sorrow,' and off he trotted with Grandad towards the gates of the zoo where they had arranged to meet the others for the picnic.

9
The Rescue Plan

All the way home on the bus 2.15 looked out of the window with a dreamy expression in his eyes.

'What's the matter with 2.15?' asked the children. 'He looks all soppy.'

'I think 'ee's in love,' said Grandad.

'In love!' said Hugh in disgust.

'Who with?' asked Gran.

'Her name is 3.45,' said 2.15 dreamily, 'and she is the most beautiful wolf in the world and we're going to live happily ever after.'

'I see,' said Gran. 'But if she's in the zoo and you're out here, how are going to manage that?'

2.15 grinned. 'I have a plan. Grandad and the lads are going to help me.'

'No way,' said Grandad. 'You forget it, 2.15. Whatever it is you're thinkin', you just forget it.'

Soon they were back home and the children were delivered to their parents. Back at the flat Grandad, Gran and Lucy sat down to a supper of beefburgers, peas and jacket potatoes. Gran laid a place for 2.15, but he just lay by the fire and looked into the flames.

'I'm not hungry,' he said. 'I don't need food, I've got love instead.'

'Come on, 2.15,' said Gran. 'You must eat, and it's your favourite.'

'No,' said the wolf. 'Not a morsel will cross my lips till he agrees to help me rescue my beloved 3.45.'

'Be reasonable, 2.15,' said Grandad. 'How can I rescue a wolf?'

'Using all the skill, ingenuity, bravery and cunning you used to blow up that enemy petrol container in the war, and when you smuggled that secret agent out of France, and when you stole those secret plans about enemy troop location and missile sites. That's how.'

'That was all a long time ago,' said Grandad sadly. 'None of us is up to that any more.'

'Not that long ago,' replied 2.15. 'If you and the lads got fit and used all your experience to think up a plan, I bet you could come up with something in no time.'

'Wartime is different, 2.15. I'm a law abidin' man, I always 'ave been and I'm not goin' to change my ways at my time of life, and that's that.'

'In that case,' announced 2.15, 'If she can't come out of the zoo to be with me, then I shall go into the zoo to be with her.'

'Oh 2.15,' protested Gran, 'don't even think of that. You'd hate it.'

'That is true,' agreed the wolf, 'but if Grandad won't help me then I shall have no choice.' He lay down by the fire and went to sleep.

'I s'pose we might as well go to bed, love,' said Grandad, and he and Gran went off to bed feeling guilty and miserable.

The next morning when they woke up, 2.15 was cooking breakfast and singing.

'Morning all,' he said as he poured the fruit juice into glasses. 'How do you want your eggs – boiled, fried sunny side up, scrambled or poached?'

'You're in a good mood this morning,' said Gran, feeling a mixture of relief and suspicion.

89

'That I am,' agreed the wolf. 'I borrowed Grandad's address book last night and phoned the lads. I explained the situation and you have been completely outvoted on the issue.'

2.15 got out his notebook. 'First I phoned Ted Walker, who wants to help – says it will make him feel young again. Then I phoned Paddy O'Connor who says it sounds like a laugh and he's game, and then, let's see, yes, the next person I got in touch with was Fred Smith who's going to be in hospital, but will send a contribution. Then I phoned Lew Solomons and he said he didn't hold with that sort of thing, but then he phoned back and said OK, because when he'd told his missis it was about true love she'd told him to help. Then I phoned Taffy Evans and he said that after all the help I'd given him with his accounts he'd be glad to help. So that only left Bill Andrews and he was out, but he rang back this morning and said that if the rest of the lads were for it so was he, "one for all and all for one" he said – so that only leaves you objecting.'

Grandad scratched his head. 'It doesn't seem right, 2.15.'

'Helping to free 3.45 so that we can live happily ever after would be a wonderful thing to do.'

'It's all well and good, 2.15, but supposin' we get caught – then we're for it.'

'We won't get caught, not with experienced soldiers like you. Anyway, no one will be expecting a wolf to get kidnapped.'

'OK. How are we going to do it,' asked Grandad with a sigh.

'The lads are coming round tonight to discuss it,' said 2.15.

'Oh,' said Grandad.

'I suppose you'll be bringing her back here. No one bothers to ask me how I feel about having a wolf in the house,' complained Gran.

'You didn't mind having me,' said 2.15, pouring the tea.

'Well, you're different,' said Gran. 'You're not a real wolf.'

'Not a *real* wolf?' exclaimed 2.15, turning the bacon over. 'Whatever do you mean?'

'You know,' replied Gran, 'you coming out of a story and all, and talking and not eating people. It makes a difference. How do I know that this 3.45 won't go off and eat all the neighbours?'

'Eat old Grubb?' said 2.15, putting butter on the toast. 'No, she won't do that. He's too scrawny.'

'Well, what *will* she eat?' demanded Gran.

2.15 served up the bacon and egg. 'Meat, I suppose,' he said.

'I can't afford meat every day,' said Gran firmly. 'Not the price it is.'

'Don't worry about money, ma'am,' said 2.15. 'I'll take care of that – from now on the Lucy Jones and her Amazing Performing Dog Show will be giving regular shows, five times a day.'

'I don't know,' continued Gran. 'We won't be able to talk to her like we do to you, and she's never lived anywhere except the zoo, she won't be at all domesticated.'

'Just think what a nice change it will be for her to be here,' said 2.15.

'That might well be, but how do you know that she won't turn out to be very vicious?'

'Madam, you are talking of the wolf I love,' said 2.15 crossly.

'Well, I'm not happy about it,' continued Gran. 'And

I want both of you out of here as soon as possible. We're not supposed to have one dog, never mind two.'

'One thing at a time, love,' said Grandad. 'Let's rescue this wolf first and then decide on the next step.'

As soon as Lucy got up, 2.15 made her breakfast and then informed her that the Lucy Jones and her Amazing Performing Dog Show was going to be performing very regularly, and would she hurry up and get dressed so that they could get on with it.

Lucy yawned. 'Why are we going to perform, 2.15?' she asked.

'Because,' explained the wolf, 'I need the money to buy meat for 3.45 once she's rescued. And I want to get some money for Gran and Grandad too, so that they can get a cottage and have a garden and live near you and your mum and dad and near me and 3.45 in the forest.'

'You could never make that much money, 2.15,' said Gran. 'It's a nice thought, but you couldn't do it.'

'Madam,' said the wolf, 'you haven't seen the Lucy Jones and her Amazing Performing Dog Show.'

'But 2.15, we'll have to go every day if we're going to make that much money,' wailed Lucy.

'And every evening,' announced 2.15, 'except tonight, when the lads are coming round to arrange the rescue of 3.45.'

'I'll never be able to watch *any* telly,' Lucy complained bitterly.

'Child, child,' exclaimed the wolf, putting his head in his paws. 'What words from one so young. What is television compared to helping 3.45, and your grandparents, and me, and seeing life and being out in the world?'

'I prefer it,' said Lucy.

'You,' said 2.15, 'are a very silly girl. Now come on, time for us to be off.'

So 2.15 and Lucy spent the day going round parks and outdoor pubs putting on shows of the Lucy Jones and her Amazing Performing Dog Show, and they made a lot of money.

That night Lucy fell exhausted into bed, but 2.15 was full of energy and insisted on cooking supper for the lads. Soon 2.15, Grandad, Ted Walker, Paddy O'Connor, Lew Solomons, Taffy Evans and Bill Andrews were sitting round the table and planning the rescue of 3.45. It was agreed that every morning Paddy O'Connor would fetch all the lads in his van and that they would go jogging round Regent's Park to get fit, and at the same time take a look at the wolf's enclosure. 2.15 was to come with them and to explain to 3.45 and the other wolves what the plan was. Before the lads left they drank a toast to comradeship and true love and living happily ever after.

So every morning 2.15 and the lads exercised in Regent's Park. At first they felt very exhausted but then they got used to it. 2.15 had long chats to 3.45 and was very happy. The date for the rescue was fixed and the other wolves agreed to help.

Each day Lucy and 2.15 went out and performed wherever there was a gathering of people, at bus queues, at shopping centres, in parks and squares, and every day they made more money. 2.15 split the money four ways, most for Grandad's house, some for 3.45's food, a bit for Lucy, and some for 'The 2.15 Guitar Fund'.

'What do you want a guitar for?' asked Lucy.

'Just want one, that's all,' replied the wolf.

Late one night everyone had gone to bed and 2.15

decided to take a bath. Soon Grandad was woken up by
the wolf carolling,

> 'I'm in love, I'm in love,
> I'm in love, I'm in love.
> I'm in love with a wonderful wolf.'

Grandad stuck his head round the bathroom door.
'Can it, 2.15. People are trying to sleep.'

'Ah yes,' said 2.15, 'but lovers don't need to sleep,'
and scrubbing his back with a brush, he sang at the top
of his voice,

> 'Falling in love again,
> What a thing to do,
> Da, dar, de, dum-dum, Can't help it.'

'You've got to stop it,' yelled Grandad. 'If you expect
me to get up early in the morning and go running, I
need some sleep.'

'Oh 3.45, I love you,' sang 2.15, not listening to anything Grandad was saying.

'I'm always dreaming of you,
De, da, de, de, de, da, de, de, de, de
I love you, my 3.45.'

'I can't stand it,' yelled Grandad, 'I need me sleep.'

At that moment the front door bell rang.

'Blow me,' said Grandad, 'I bet you've gone and woken up Pete Grubb.'

'Who cares?' said 2.15 carelessly. 'All the world loves a lover.'

'I don't,' said Grandad. 'Not at one in the morning I don't, and I bet Grubb doesn't either.'

'Don't worry,' said 2.15, leaping out of the bath and wrapping a towel round himself, 'I'll explain,' and before Grandad could stop him, 2.15 had flung the front door open. There stood Pete Grubb, half asleep in his dressing gown.

'Now look here, Bert. . . .' he began and then, seeing who was standing before him, his voice trailed off.

'Pete, Pete,' said 2.15 cheerfully, putting his wet paws on Pete Grubb's shoulders, 'my old friend Pete. I'm in love, isn't that wonderful?'

Pete Grubb looked past 2.15 at Grandad, who was standing in the hall wondering what on earth to do.

'I had a funny vision, Bert. I thought a wet wolf draped in a towel answered the door and kissed me and said he was in love.'

Grandad went to the door and supported Pete Grubb. 'Come on Pete, back to bed with you. You were havin' a bad dream. 'Ere, let me take you back to your own place.'

'Thanks Bert,' said Pete Grubb. 'It must be some-

thing they put in the beer down at the pub. I've been saying for ages it doesn't taste like it used to. I'll complain, I'll get the law on to them, you just see if I don't.'

'You do that, Pete,' said Grandad, helping him into bed. 'And no more bad dreams about wolves.'

'Hope not, Bert,' said Pete Grubb.

'Night, now,' said Grandad, and he crept out, turning off the light.

When Grandad got back into the flat, 2.15 was cleaning the bath singing, 'Love is the sweetest thing. . . .'

'Now you stop that, mate,' said Grandad firmly. 'If you don't calm down, the rescue of your wolf is off. I can't stand another night like this one.'

'Fear not, comrade-in-arms,' said 2.15. 'I shall not

sing the praises of my loved one any longer. I shall sleep and prepare for the rigours that lie ahead on the morrow.' And 2.15 lay down and went to sleep.

''Ee'll 'ave to go,' Grandad told Gran as he got back into bed. 'If it goes on like this, I'll go round the bend.'

'It's not for much longer,' Gran reassured him. 'Once you've got 3.45 out of the zoo, he'll be off to the forest and that will be the end of that.'

''Ee says 'ee's going to get the money for us to get that cottage in the country,' said Grandad wistfully.

'I wouldn't put it past him,' said Gran. 'He'll be so grateful if you do rescue 3.45.'

The next day the lads did their training in Regent's Park and, as soon as it was over, 2.15 went off with Lucy for several performances of The Lucy Jones and her Amazing Performing Dog Show. When they got home at about four, Lucy flopped down exhausted and turned on the TV. 2.15 busied himself counting the money they'd made.

'Look at that,' he said to Lucy proudly. 'We *are* doing well. We've already got more than £5,000 towards Grandad's cottage.'

'Great,' said Lucy listlessly as she lay back, utterly exhausted.

'I know,' agreed 2.15. 'Come on, let's not waste time. Let's go out and busk for the film queues. There's not long to go now and not a minute to be wasted.'

'I've had enough,' said Lucy, 'and my feet hurt. Leave me alone, I want to watch telly.'

'But Lucy, the cottage, think about the cottage.'

'I'm tired, 2.15. Let me watch my programme.'

'The telly, the telly, the telly, that's all you think of,' said 2.15 angrily, turning the TV off. 'Now put on your anorak and let's be off. We've got money to earn.'

'Go away,' yelled Lucy, putting the TV back on. 'I want to watch the telly.'

'Well you can't,' said 2.15, and he snatched the TV up and threw it out of the window.

'2.15,' shouted Lucy in horror, 'it might hit someone.'

Together they rushed to the window. There on the ground lay the TV, crushed to smithereens.

'Thank goodness,' said Lucy. 'No one was down there.'

'Oh dear,' said 2.15. 'I was a bit hasty. What do you think will happen?'

'I don't know,' said Lucy. 'We'd better phone Liz Howes, she'll know what to do.' So she phoned the social worker.

'2.15 threw the telly out of the window,' said Lucy. 'No, I'm not kidding, he really did. No one was hurt, but we don't know what to do.'

'That wolf is becoming a menace,' said Liz Howes. 'Look, you hang on. I'll bring my TV round and then if anyone starts trying to find out who did it, at least you'll have a TV and be covered.'

'Don't let Pete Grubb see you come in the door with a telly,' said Lucy.

'Don't worry, I'll think of something,' replied Liz Howes.

A few minutes later Liz Howes turned up wheeling a pram with the TV hidden under a blanket.

'Hello, Miss Howes,' said Pete Grubb, putting his head round the door. 'I didn't know you had a baby.'

'It's not mine, Mr Grubb. I'm helping out a friend, and Lucy is going to keep an eye on the baby for me.'

'I like babies,' said Pete Grubb. 'Can I have a peep?'

'Another day,' said Liz Howes. 'He's teething and is

a bit grumpy just now,' and she quickly pushed the pram into Lucy's flat.

As she unloaded the TV Liz Howes said to 2.15, 'Much as I love you, I think it's time you went home.'

'I know, I know,' agreed the wolf. 'I'm sorry about the TV but it's very desperate. I've got to make lots of money for Grandad's cottage and there's not much time left before I go off to live happily ever after.'

Lucy told Liz why 2.15 had thrown the telly out of the window.

'Alright,' said Liz Howes, 'I will come with you in the evenings, 2.15, and it will be the Liz Howes and her Amazing Performing Dog Show. That will make a nice change for me from social work. However, you must stop doing crazy things and calm down, or you won't stay free long enough to rescue 3.45.'

'Forgive me,' said 2.15. 'I have indeed been foolish, but from now on my behaviour will be beyond reproach, while I wait for a lifetime of bliss with my 3.45.'

Happy Ever After

As the day for 3.45's rescue got closer, 2.15 began to read books of wartime exploits to get ideas for the rescue. Eventually he came up with a plan and explained it to the lads. They all agreed that it sounded good, and Tuesday was fixed as the great night. That night, when the lads left, 2.15 went downstairs with them and didn't come back.

'Where's 'ee gorn?' asked Grandad.

'Don't know,' said Gran, 'but he does often go out late. I sometimes hear him coming baek.'

'I don't know where 'ee gets the energy,' said Grandad, turning on the TV news. 'Training in the morning with us, the performing dog show all day and in the evening, and then off again at night. I 'ope 'ee's not gettin' up to any mischief.'

The news came on and after a few items on the world situation, the newsreader said that there had been strange reports coming in from people living near the zoo, about someone dressed up as a wolf who had been seen playing the guitar and singing outside the zoo. This strange person was preventing the residents from sleeping and the police would be looking for the offender.

'2.15!' cried Grandad.

'So that's where he has been going,' said Gran. 'Serenading his true love.'

''Ee's barmy these days,' said Grandad, ''ee really is. 'Ee's in dead trouble now. The police will pick 'im up, sure as eggs is eggs.'

'There's not much we can do,' said Gran.

'If 'ee gets caught, then the rescue will be off,' said Grandad. 'That would be a shame. I'd quite got into the idea – I'd be sorry if we 'ad to call it off.'

'Poor 2.15,' said Gran. 'Just when he was so happy.'

'Yeah,' agreed Grandad. 'And in the end 'is undoing 'ad nothing to do with Pete Grubb.'

'He must have used some of the money he collected to buy a guitar,' Gran said.

''Ee's done very well on the collection,' said Grandad. 'There's enough to buy us that cottage, love.'

'Yes,' sighed Gran. 'He was pretty fantastic.'

Suddenly the door bell rang and there stood Liz Howes and 2.15.

'I heard the same news,' explained Liz, 'so I leapt into my car and got there just before the police. We had to leave the guitar in our hurry.'

'Why are you taking so many risks, 2.15?' asked Grandad.

'It's a case of stars in your eyes with him,' said Gran. 'Isn't that right, 2.15, you keep getting carried away?'

'You've put your finger right on the point, ma'am,' said 2.15. 'I've been on my own for so long, I'm over-excited.'

'Well, you've got to stop it,' said Grandad. 'In a few days we'll have 3.45 out of there and you'll both be back in your forest, and then you can live happily ever after. But you must promise me and cross your 'eart not to do anything wild in the meantime, 'cos I can't take it.'

'Sorry,' said 2.15, 'I really am, I just didn't think. Nothing was further from mind than causing anxiety and distress. Indeed, my first priority at all times is the maintainence of the peace, well-being and equilibrium of your home and. . . .'

'Alright 2.15,' said Gran, 'we get the idea. Now let's have an early night, another long day tomorrow.'

After that everything went peacefully until the evening of 3.45's rescue.

The lads turned up, dressed all in black, with black on their faces too. They were very excited. Grandad got out a map of the zoo and put it up on the wall with bluetak, and he explained to everyone what their role in the 'Operation Wolf' was.

2.15 told the lads how grateful he was and announced that he had made so much money from The Amazing Performing Dog Show that he could give Grandad a cheque for £25,000, and that he had £500 for each of the lads to take a holiday with. He gave each of them an envelope with the money in. Toasts were drunk and everyone was happy.

At the arranged time the lads and 2.15 set off. 'Operation Wolf' went off with military precision and by 2 a.m. 3.45 was lying in front of Gran's fire with 2.15 holding her paw tenderly. 3.45 whispered something in 2.15's ear and he smiled and said, 'She wants me to say how grateful she is to you for her rescue.'

'You just tell 'er,' said Grandad, 'that I 'aven't 'ad so much fun in years, and that it's a pleasure 'aving her 'ere.'

'Come on,' said Gran. 'Time for bed. It's late, so we'll have a nice lie-in tomorrow morning.'

The next morning 2.15 took 3.45 into Lucy's bedroom to meet Lucy. Lucy looked hard at the wolf and put her head under the sheets.

'What's wrong?' asked 2.15.

'She's a real wolf,' said Lucy.

'Yes, of course she is,' agreed 2.15. 'But you don't have to worry. She's never even heard of Red Riding

102

Hood. Don't worry, I'll see you're alright.'

Lucy peeped out from behind the sheet. 3.45 was staring at her.

'3.45 wants me to thank you for bringing me out of the forest and to London, so that we could fall in love and she could get rescued.'

'I didn't exactly bring you,' said Lucy. 'You just sort of came.'

'Still, she's very grateful,' said 2.15.

Lucy smiled at the wolf and put out her hand. 3.45 trotted up and licked Lucy's hand, and then she went and sat by 2.15.

'Well, I think she's a very lucky wolf,' said Lucy, "cos she's got you and you're the very best wolf in the world, except when you throw my telly out of the window.'

'Don't even mention that,' said 2.15. 'I feel silly whenever I think about it.'

'As soon as I've had breakfast,' said Lucy, 'I'll take you both to the park.'

So while Lucy munched her breakfast, 2.15 explained to 3.45 about going for walks. Soon the three of them were walking along the High Road in the direction of the park. Coming towards them was Pete Grubb.

'Morning, Mr Grubb,' said Lucy cheerfully. 'No more bad dreams?'

'You've got two of them now,' said Pete Grubb. 'You're not allowed to keep one dog, and now you've got two. I'll tell on you lot, you won't get away with this.'

3.45 barred her teeth, and Lucy pulled at the leads as they dashed off.

In the park 2.15 and 3.45 went for a walk, and when they returned 2.15 told Lucy that 3.45 didn't like the city and was scared of cars and traffic. She even wanted to eat Pete Grubb. 2.15 thought they should all go back to the forest as soon as possible.

'We'll talk to Grandad when we get back,' promised Lucy. They went home the long way to avoid too much traffic since it scared 3.45.

When they got back to the flat Lucy told Grandad that 3.45 wanted to leave London.

'That's all well and good,' said Grandad, 'but the whole of the London Police Force is lookin' for her,' and he held out a newspaper with a headline: 'Wolf Stolen from London Zoo'.

'And it was all on the news,' said Gran.

'Maybe I shouldn't have taken 2.15 and 3.45 out for a walk,' said Lucy.

'Don't suppose it matters,' said Grandad, 'providing you didn't meet old Grubb.'

'I did,' said Lucy.

'Yes,' said 2.15. 'He seemed alright. Carried on about there being two of us and the usual stuff about reporting you and getting you into trouble.'

So later that day there was a Council of War. All the lads were there, and Liz Howes, Grandad, Gran, Lucy and 2.15.

Gran started the proceedings. 'We've got to get 2.15 and 3.45 out of London, but it said on the news that police were searching for the lost wolf and many roads out of London were being checked.'

'What we need to get 3.45 and 2.15 home in is a car that the police won't check,' said Lucy.

'A police car,' suggested 2.15.

'But none of us is in the police,' said Grandad.

'Well, what else wouldn't the police check?' asked 2.15.

'Don't suppose they'd check anything military,' said Taffy Evans.

'You could borrow a tank,' suggested 2.15.

'Don't be daft,' snapped Grandad. 'Any other suggestions?'

'An ambulance,' suggested Liz Howes.

'Yes,' commented Grandad. 'It's an idea, but we 'aven't got one.'

'I know,' said Gran. 'A security van.'

'But we 'aven't got one of them, either,' said Grandad.

'I know that,' said Gran, 'but Pete Grubb drives one, and it's down there in the yard now.'

'Grubb would never agree to take them, love,' said Grandad.

'Don't ask him,' said Gran. 'Just put them in there, and then I'm sure 2.15 can persuade Pete to take him to the forest.'

'Ma'am,' said 2.15 grinning widely, 'it would be a pleasure.'

Everyone agreed that it was a wonderful idea and that Lucy should go with them just in case anything went wrong.

Soon afterwards Grandad knocked on Pete Grubb's door. A few moments later it was opened.

'Oh, it's you, Bert. I was just going to sleep. I'm working the night shift.'

'Sorry Pete, didn't mean to keep you awake. What time are you goin' on duty then?'

'7 o'clock,' said Pete Grubb.

'Alright,' said Grandad, 'I'll talk to you about the dogs another time.'

'You've got no business having those dogs,' said Pete Grubb. 'They can't go soon enough as far as I'm concerned.' And he slammed the door.

Grandad grinned and went back into his own flat. "Is shift starts at 7 o'clock, 'ee's asleep now and the keys are in the pocket of 'is jacket, 'anging on the kitchen door. The kitchen window is open.'

'Say no more,' said 2.15 and he ambled out, returning five minutes later with the keys.

'Right,' said Grandad. 'Well, let's put you lot in the van. Gran will make up a picnic and I'll find you some cards and a few books so you don't get bored.'

'So the plan is,' said 2.15, 'that we go and wait for Grubb in the van, and when he gets in I persuade him in the nicest possible way to take us home.'

'The only problem might be people seeing us getting into the van,' said Lucy.

'We need a sideshow,' said Paddy O'Connor. 'When we were in the commandos and we were going to blow something up or whatever, we always created a diversion.'

'What kind of diversion?'

'A fire, a riot, a fight, something like that.'

'I know,' said Lucy. 'Let's get the kids to help. They all love 2.15 and they'd be glad to help. They can all make a rumpus out in the front, while we get in the van at the back.'

So all the children from the flats were fetched, and they were delighted to be told to make as much noise as they could and to behave as badly as possible.

'Right,' said Grandad, 'they don't want to be in the van for too long, so at 4 o'clock the kids make the diversion, then 2.15, 3.45 and Lucy and I will nip downstairs. I'll open the van, they'll 'op in and I'll lock them in. Then I'll throw the keys through Grubb's window and 'ee'll think 'ee dropped them on the floor.'

'Great,' said 2.15.

So at 4 o'clock Lucy said, 'Let the rumpus begin,' and Hugh pulled Maureen's hair, Maureen kicked him, Doreen screamed for her mum, Mike threw mud at Sue and soon the other kids in the flats joined in. While all this was going on Grandad, 2.15, 3.45 and Lucy slipped out. 2.15 gave Gran a big hug and kiss.

'See you soon,' said 2.15, 'in the cottage in the country. Don't be too long in coming.'

'We won't,' said Gran. 'And good luck. We'll know what happens, Lucy will phone us as soon as she's home. We'll just sit here by the phone and wait for news.'

By the time the rumpus was over, the three were firmly locked up in the van. 2.15 explained to 3.45 what was happening in wolf language and she nodded.

'She was born in the zoo,' explained 2.15. 'She's not used to this sort of thing.'

Pete Grubb came down at 6.30 and got into the van and drove off. 2.15 leaned over the seat and put his head on Grubb's shoulder.

'OK Grubb, this is a stick-up. Just keep driving.'

'Have you got a gun?' asked Pete Grubb.

'No,' replied 2.15, 'but I've got lots of teeth, most of them wound round your left ear, so if you don't do what I want you to do, I'll just give it a little bite,' and 2.15 licked Pete Grubb's ear. 'Hmmm, delicious,' he muttered.

'You're a wolf, aren't you?' said Pete Grubb.

'*A* wolf!' said 2.15. 'I am *the* wolf, the wolf out of Red Riding Hood.'

'You mean old Bert wasn't having me on all those weeks ago.'

'No, he told you the gospel truth. Now, in the back

here with me are Lucy and my wife, 3.45, who recently gave up her residence at the zoo.'

'You mean I've got two wolves in this van?'

'That's it,' said 2.15. 'And I love ears, so you drive carefully and don't say anything unfortunate to anyone.'

'What do you want?' said Pete Grubb.

'We want to go back home. Lucy knows the way, she'll tell you how to get there.'

'I'll get the law on you when all this is over,' fumed Pete Grubb.

'No you won't,' said 2.15. 'No one would believe you, they'd all think you were mad.'

'So it was you in the flat all the time?' said Pete Grubb bitterly.

'Right on,' agreed the wolf.

'And it was you at the football match?'

'Yup,' said the wolf.

'And it was you that kissed me on both cheeks the other night?'

'It certainly was,' said 2.15.

'I'll get my own back,' fumed Pete Grubb. 'You see if I don't.'

Despite all his protests, Pete Grubb drove them to Lucy's home. Lucy's mum and dad had been warned and the travellers were warmly greeted when they arrived. 2.15 said hello to everyone, and then he and 3.45 ran off into the forest. Pete Grubb sat in a disgruntled heap by the fire.

'A talking wolf,' he said. 'Who would have guessed?'

'No one,' agreed Lucy. 'It was an unlikely story. You alright, Mr Grubb? You look ill.'

'I feel ill,' said Pete Grubb.

'I'll phone your firm and explain you're ill,' said Lucy's mum. 'And I'll take you over to my neighbour who's got a spare room.'

So Pete Grubb went to stay with the neighbour who was a widow. But poor Pete Grubb didn't get any better. Each morning when he woke up the windows of his room were wide open and his 'flu got worse and worse.

'He's such a nice man,' the widow told Lucy's mum, 'and he needs looking after. But you know, it's very odd, each night I shut the windows and each morning they're open again. Who can be doing it I can't imagine.'

'I think I'd better go and talk to 2.15,' said Lucy. 'For some reason he wants to keep Pete Grubb in the forest.'

'Can you think why?' asked her mother.

'No,' said Lucy, 'but you never know with 2.15.'

So Lucy put on her red anorak and went walking in the forest. There was a rustling in the undergrowth and 2.15 jumped out.

'Hello,' he said. 'Remember me? I am your destiny and you are my dinner.'

'Oh there you are, 2.15,' said Lucy. 'I was looking for you.'

'For me! Why?'

'I want to know why you keep opening Pete Grubb's window at night.'

'Oh that,' said 2.15. 'It's so he can live happily ever after.'

'I don't get it,' said Lucy.

'All that television has addled your mind,' commented the wolf. 'He's got to stay in the forest a bit longer. He must marry the widow and then they'll both be happy and he'll stop being so horrible to everyone.'

'But 2.15, this isn't a fairy story, this is life.'

'Ah but *my* life *is* a fairy story, and Pete Grubb is part of my life, and therefore he too must live happily ever after. He has no choice in the matter. Don't worry, I'll fix it all up. Don't forget to tell me when Gran and Grandad get their cottage,' and off he scampered, clicking his heels in the air as he ran.

When Lucy got back home she told her mum about 2.15's motives.

'You won't believe it, Mum, he wants Pete Grubb and the widow to live happily ever after.'

'Well, he seems to have succeeded,' said her mother. 'Look.'

Lucy looked out of the window and there was Pete Grubb, sitting in the garden, holding the neighbour's

hand and smiling into her eyes.

'Well,' said Lucy. 'He looks quite nice, not like the horrible old Grubb at all. You know, Mum, he's quite special, that wolf. He changed my life, and Gran and Grandad's and lots of other people in the flats' lives, and now Pete Grubb's too – I'm glad he mistook me for Red Riding Hood. Think of all the fun I'd have missed if he hadn't. I'd still be watching TV all the time.'

'Do you prefer helping people to live happily ever after?' asked her mother.

'I most certainly do,' said Lucy. 'That is really a good thing to be doing.'